Journee & Juelz
A Dope Hood Love
Written By: Nikki Nicole

Acknowledgements

Hey you guys. I'm Authoress Nikki Nicole some of you may know me and some of you don't. I'm introducing myself. This is my sixth book. I wanted to get this novella out for a really long time. I love this story. I originally started writing this book in December of last year.

I was in really good writing space while writing this. Journee Leigh Armstrong and Juelz Thomas have been a pleasure to pen. They have their own stance. I was a little skeptical about them because they're new kids on the block. I have received great feedback about them. I hope you guys love it.

I want to thank God for giving me this gift to share with you. Without this him there is no me. I want to thank my supporters I appreciate each one of you guys. I always say if it's something that you want to do in life please do it. Step out on faith you have nothing to lose and everything to gain. I'll support you because you supported me and I'll help you because you helped me.

It's time for my **S/O Sonya**, **Samantha**, **Tatina**, **Asha**, **PinkDiva**, **Padrica**, **Chamyka**, **Darletha**, **Trecie**, **Valentina**, **Troy**, **Pat**, **Crystal**, **Reneshia**, **Toi**, **Ella**, **Ava**, **Snowie**, **Bacia**, **Sherelle**, **Shawn**, **Denetta**, **Blany**, **Catherine**, **Jawanda**, **Jennifer**, **Sherre** these ladies right here are a hot mess. I love them to death. They go so hard about these books it doesn't make any sense. I have to run and hide sometimes.

If you're looking for us meet us in Nikki Nicole's Readers Trap on Facebook we are live and indirect all day.

S/O to My Pen Bae's **Ash ley**, **Chyna L**, **Ashley Robinson**, **Quanna Lashae**, **T. Miles**, **Brittany Pitteard**, I love them to the moon and back head over to Amazon and grab a book by them also.

To my new readers I have two complete series available

Baby I Play for Keeps Series

For My Savage, I Will Ride or Die Series

Join my readers group **Nikki Nicole's Readers Trap on Facebook**

Follow me on **Facebook Nikki Taylor**

Instagram **@WatchNikkiwrite**

email me *authoressnikkinicole@gmail.com*

Join my email contact list for exclusive sneak peeks. *http://eepurl.com/czCbKL*

Contents

If It's Meant to Be, Eventually We'll Find Our Way Back To Each Other...

Chapter 1- Journee

Oh my God it was Tuesday afternoon. I'm tired as fuck. I stayed in the trap all night until about 3:00am, it was a good night. I made seven thousand in three hours. I still managed to make it to school on time and focus. I'm a clock watcher and I've been watching the clock all day.

I had shit to do and moves to make. School was dragging and the block was hot as fuck. It was early March school finally let out thank God. I was ready to go. All the dope boys were riding past the school house blasting their music and showing off their whips begging to bag a couple of chicks.

I wasn't impressed that shit didn't excite me. I was too busy trying to get my own and provide for my family. The weather was nice, warm and humid. Of course, the girls were dressed in their best summer attire trying to bait a nigga also. It was the beginning of Spring and the weather was funny acting. One day it was hot and the next day it was cold.

Today the Georgia heat wasn't a joke. As soon as the bell rang, I flew out of the double doors and headed home. I was in a rush too. I walked in a very fast pace. I needed to start dinner early. I laid out the pack of meat that I intended on cooking this morning before I left. It should be un thawed by the time I make it home.

***

I made it home in about fifteen minutes, the house phone was ringing already, I already knew it was my best friend Nikki calling. I didn't have a chance to holler at her when school let out. My phone was still off. I didn't believe in having my phone on during school it was a distraction.

I couldn't answer right now because, I had to get dinner started. If I picked the phone up I wouldn't get anything done. I didn't have time to talk right now. I'll hit her back in a few after I'm finished with everything. Nine times out of ten I'll see her later and we can chop it up then.

I just started preparing dinner for my two siblings, my mom was sick with her ovarian cancer so she couldn't cook. Everything was on me. I needed my brother and sister to hurry up and get home from school, eat, do homework, and go to bed, so I could sneak out the house and bleed the block.

I hooked up with an upcoming dope boy on the rise named Juelz Thomas he was from Miami, Florida he's been in Atlanta for about five years now. I sold dope for him at one of his trap houses on Simpson Rd.

Khadijah and Khadir would be home from school any minute now. I had to finish my homework and help Khadijah with hers. She's in middle school and she swear her math is to hard. I think she's just not paying attention that's her problem. Khadir was in elementary school, my little brother was so smart he didn't need anybody helping him with his homework.

It was a great day at Frederick Douglass High School (Doug) today. No fights, no fussing everything was cool. I wanted to start a food fight with the slop they piled on my lunch plate.

"Journee, baby is you here?" My mother asked in her sweet voice.

"Yes mother, I'm here. I'm starting dinner, do you need me to do something for you?" I asked. I would never call my mother mama; she gets the highest respect from me. Right before she turned ill she was the best mother a girl could ask for and she still is.

A lot of things in our household has changed because my mother's income has been reduced drastically she's only getting disability and food stamps but that's cool because if she keeps the bills paid and a roof over our head I'll handle the rest.

"Yes, come here for a minute, I need to ask you a few things." My mother stated.

"Here I come, let me cut the stove down."

"Hurry up," my mother yelled. I may be sick but I'm not crazy. Journee is getting money from somewhere, I know she's not getting it from me.

"Yes mother?" I asked and smiled. I wonder what my mother could want, I was already making her some tea.

"Come here Journee, sit down for a minute. Let me speak with you for a few minutes, I know things are tight around here. I'm not able to provide for you three like I should, but where in the fuck are you getting this extra money from, and don't say Valerie has been buying you stuff because, I called her earlier and asked her and she said no." My mother revealed.

"Let me explain." I pleaded. *Damn I'm fucked but I rather keep it real than lie.*

"You got five fucking minutes." My mother sassed and rolled her neck.

"Mother."

"Mother my ass. Journee, you think that your ass is slick. I know that you've been sneaking out of the house as soon as you think I'm sleep to go up on Simpson Rd. and hang out with the dope boys." My mother revealed.

"I'm looking out for Juelz and Skeet in case the police come. They're paying me to look out, that's where the extra money is coming from." I blurted. *I just flat out lied to my mother, I couldn't let her know that I was hustling out here in these streets.*

"Journee Leigh Armstrong, are you actually about to sit here and lie in my damn face. I know I'm not who I used to be as far as health wise, but please don't get this shit confused. I will bust you in your ass and forget that you're my daughter.

You have over three thousand dollars in a shoe box. You have four ounces of pure coke stuffed in your drawer in your socks. I can't believe you. Yes, I went through all your stuff. I'm so disappointed in you.

Let me enlighten you a little bit, the streets are a dead end you either die or go to jail, look at your father for instance. Journee those crackers gave him a hundred years for drugs and conspiracy. He died in prison he never got the chance to know you, do you think that I want that for you?

I want you to be fucking no great, no the best, I refuse to let you be a statistic, what can you do different with drug money that anybody else couldn't? What makes you so different?

You don't have to lie to me Journee, you ain't looking out for Juelz you are serving. I watched you do that shit with my own two green eyes." My mother chastised me.

"Mother, I'm so sorry I lied to you, I really am. I need the money you know how hard I've been looking for a job so things won't be so tight around here.

Every job I applied for, they chose another candidate. I must face reality, when you leave this world momma, it's just me and my brother and sister. Nobody is going to look out for us they ain't doing it now. Khadijah and Khadir are growing every day. I'm not doing this for me. I'm doing it for us."

"Journee, cut the bullshit, When I leave this world you guys will be great, I have insurance policy for $500,000 that's more than enough for you guys to survive. I have social security and a pension check that you'll receive every month once I pass away. You have a lot of excuses for what you are doing but no solutions, answer my question what can you do different?" My mother argued.

"I'm not waiting for you to pass away mother, to reap the benefits from your hard work."

"Journee Leigh Armstrong, answer my question before I put my fucking hands on you little girl." My mother was yelling all up in my face.

"I'm using the money to open my own restaurant and attend culinary school," I cried.

"Journee Leigh, come here, stop crying, I don't agree with what you are doing, but I can't stop you, what if something happens to you? All I ask is that you make the right decisions. If I leave this world today and you get caught selling drugs who's going to look after Khadijah and Khadir? They'll be property of the state. Think about that." My mother continued to chastise me.

"Mother, I'm sorry I'm going to stop." I cried.

"Stop crying Journee because when you were posted up on the block you weren't crying. Everything was all good until you got caught. I never raised you to lie. I didn't raise you that way. All money ain't good money. When it's your time it's your time be patient things will change." My mother explained.

"Yes mam."

"Alright don't ever bring that shit up in my house again. I don't condone that shit. Contact Juelz or Skeet so they can get this stuff out of my house right now." My mother continued to chastise me.

Julissa

Lord, what am I doing wrong? What am I going to do with this child of mine? I raised my child the best way I knew how. I know things are tight around here. The problem with our children today is they feel that what you do as a parent isn't enough.

I keep a roof over your head, make sure you eat every day and I make sure your clothes and shoes are decent. I don't want to be a burden on my child at all. She has a lot of heart and she's determined just like her father. When I look at Journee, I see Julian her father. It warmed my heart when she said that she wasn't waiting on me to pass to reap my benefits.

Journee has a lot of responsibilities. She never complains about nothing that I ask her to do. She's a provider. I trained her to get it out the mud by any means necessary. I don't want her selling drugs. It dangerous that's my baby girl I love her to death and I hate when I leave this world I wouldn't be able to see her anymore.

The type of relationship that Journee and I have we are very open with each other and I trust her. She has never lied to me before but I expected her to tell me the truth not partial. I'm glad that she's going to stop. My daughter is so bright and intelligent. I'm not saying that she's better than everybody, but I didn't want her to be a trap queen like I was.

I'm loving the woman that Journee is growing up to become. I hate that she must grow up so young but hey these are the cards we were dealt. I tried to beat this ovarian cancer but this cancer is beating the shit out of me some days are better than others.

I don't know when I'll be called home but before I leave this earth. I want to instill in Journee, Khadijah, Khadir how important family is and they should stick together no matter what. At the end of the day they only have each other.

Lord knows my family ain't shit. I've been raising myself for as long as I could remember. My mother is still alive, would she raise my kids if I died hell no and I wouldn't want her too. Journee father is deceased and his relatives didn't care for me.

Khadijah and Khadir father left me for another woman that he married and he refuses to take care of his children. That's why I got Journee emancipated because she's capable to do it. She's doing a damn good job. She'll turn seventeen within the next couple of months. I know she'll be a great mother when she has her own.

Journee

I feel bad that I had to lie to my mother, It's out in the open now. I headed back to the kitchen so I could finish preparing our dinner. Spaghetti, corn on the cob and garlic bread. I heard Khadir knock on the door. I had to wipe my face I didn't want him to notice that I've been crying.

Khadijah and Khadir finally made it home from school. Dinner was still cooking. I was sitting in the living room listening to Khadijah rant about her day at school while helping her with her homework.

My mind was in another place. I couldn't even give my sister my full attention because I couldn't seem to process that my mom found out that I was selling drugs. I feel bad that I had to lie about what I was doing. She never told me to stop what I was doing; she didn't say that it was ok either. I would call Juelz later and tell him that I couldn't come to work anymore.

I would have to figure something else out because my mother was already sick and I didn't won't her stressing about me because I was hustling in these streets. I'll fall back for now. I can't even get a part time job because I must help around the house full time. I sent Juelz a text

Juelz- I can't work no more.

Journee- Why

Juelz- My mother found out

Journee- Meet me on Hollywood

Juelz- I can't

Journee- I'm coming up threw there.

Juelz said he was coming through here. I would have his stuff ready I couldn't move this work anymore. We wouldn't be working together anymore. I got finished with dinner early. Everybody was in their rooms already. I cleaned the kitchen up and straightened the living room back up.

Khadijah's lazy ass wasn't about to do shit. I read Khadir a book before he went to bed he was sleep already. I went to my mother's bedroom to see her; she was wide awake looking at TV.

"Journee Leigh Armstrong, you were about to sneak out and sell some drugs tonight. You had to check on me first." My mother laughed.

"Mother, stop I already feel bad. I really do, but I told Juelz that I'm not going to be able to do that anymore. He's coming by here in a few to pick up something."

"Yes, get that white girl the fuck up out of my house. You're on punishment. I'm proud of you Journee for making the right decision. Troubles don't last always. It gets greater later. I promise you it does." My mother stated.

"Mother what do you know about white girl?"

"More than what you know." My mother laughed.

"Enlighten me."

"I'm not because I don't want to glorify selling drugs, I know a lot about it, that's why I don't want you selling it. I'm your mother and not your friend." My mother stated.

Chapter 2-Juelz

Journee sent me a text stating that she couldn't work anymore because her mom found out she was selling drugs for me. I met Journee through my best friend Skeet he was dating Journee's best friend Nikki. Shawty approached me about a job so I decided to help her out. I didn't want her out her hustling but she insisted.

My only requirement is that she went to school every day and graduated. She did all of that. She was one of my best workers so far, she was bringing in the most money. She was a natural. I hate to lose her but it is what it is.

I wonder how and when? I wanted her to meet me on Simpson Rd. but she said she couldn't get out. I was about to slide through on her and pick up the rest of the work she had and get my plate. I was feeling Journee but she was too damn young so I kept that shit strictly business until she was of age to be with me.

***

I pulled up on Journee's block she stayed on Collier rd. I sent her a text and told her I was pulling up and to come outside. I pulled in front of her house and killed the engine. Journee took her time coming out. When she finally made it outside to the car.

I couldn't even close my mouth she had on some little as night shorts with a tank top that her breast swallowed and bonnet on her head. Her honey brown skin glistened as the moon light shed its light on her. Her big brown eyes had a beautiful glow.

Her lips were pouty and suck able. She smelled like fresh strawberries. She had the duffle bag in one hand and my plate and a soda in the other hand. She opened my car door. We locked eyes with each other.

"What's up Juelz, here's your plate and your drink. The work is in the duffle bag. You can recount and reweigh it if you want too." She stated coolly.

"Ride up the block with me to drop this bag off to Skeet, Nikki up there. You can drive while I eat."

"Juelz, I need to change clothes. I can't go nowhere looking like this." She pouted.

"You're fine ain't nobody looking at you no way. If a nigga can't accept the real you he ain't the one no way."

"That's the problem if somebody is looking I don't want them to see me like this." She laughed.

"You good Journee are you checking for somebody on the block you don't even have to get out the car? I'll run the bag in."

"I'm not checking for anybody look at me I have a bonnet on my head and my pajamas. I wasn't planning to go anywhere. I just came outside to give you your stuff and this plate." She explained.

"Um huh yes let me find out you trying to holla at one of those niggas on the block."

"Whatever Juelz, move out the way so we can go. I have school tomorrow in case you forgot. I'm not like Nikki, I don't skip school to chill on the block." She stated. She took her bonnet off and her long sandy brown hair fell down her back.

I kept catching glances at her while she was driving while I was eating my food. Journee could really cook like she was somebody mother at just the age of sixteen. We wouldn't be seeing each other anymore since she wouldn't be working for me. If Giselle caught me she would act ignorant.

Giselle is my situation we're together but we ain't. I've been kicking it with her for a little over a year. She ain't the one but she's convenient. She can fuck and suck me but she can't feed me. She can blow through my bands at the mall but if lost all she couldn't help me get it back. That's my lil situation until I make Journee mine.

Journee

I shouldn't even let Juelz talk me into coming on the block everybody in their mammy was out dying to see who the chick is pushing his Benz. He doesn't even have any tint. I don't need any extra problems or if somebody assumes I'm with him and I'm not.

Females are quick to assume some shit. Skeet came down and got the bag with his AK-47 strapped behind his back. Nikki ran to the car. Those two are inseparable.

"Journee get out." My best friend Nikki asked.

"Nikki get back, hell no she's not getting out." My former boss Juelz yelled.

"I'm headed back to the house call me in a few."

I don't know what Juelz problem was. He had an attitude because Nikki asked me to get out of the car she was being messy but I'm here for it they already know how I give it up.

"Circle the block?" He asked.

I did as I was told Juelz was making sure his work was good. I understood.

"Journee so what are you going to do now since you can't hustle?" He laughed.

"I don't know Juelz. I haven't thought about it yet. I have some money saved up."

"I got another job for you. You want it?" He asked.

"It depends on what it is."

"I got three houses that I need cleaned once a week and I need to eat every day, can you cook for me too?" He asked.

"Dang Juelz why you didn't offer me this job first? How much are you paying?"

"First, I didn't know you like that to trust you up in my shit and to eat your food. I trust you a little bit but I'm paying a thousand a week Journee is that cool with you?" He laughed.

"What's so funny Juelz my momma almost beat my ass because she found out I was selling dope. I had to lie to her about what I was doing and I never do that. I would never steal from you because you looked out for me. I'm not doing this to stunt I'm doing this to provide for my brother and sister."

"Calm down Journee I got you, you don't have to trap no more." He stated coolly.

"Where are the houses located?"

"Mableton and Kennesaw?" He stated.

"Juelz how am I supposed to get way up there without a car? I'm not riding Marta with a shit load of cleaning supplies and some groceries."

"Journee chill out you actually cute when you mad. How much money you got saved? We can go to the auction and get you a car; you already got your license. All you have to pay is your car insurance." He laughed.

"I got fifteen thousand saved why? It's in the bank and I got three thousand at the crib. My insurance gone be high as fuck Juelz because I'm not even eighteen yet did you forget?"

"You got enough money to get something nice; you need about sixty-five hundred to get something real nice."

"You owe me three thousand for my services for this week and if you want me to start work next week add a thousand to that, but I don't need anything flashy. I can get Maxima or Camry."

"If I'm putting the rest with it than you'll get whatever I pick out." He stated.

"Whatever Juelz in that case I'll bring my sixty-eight hundred."

I pulled up at my house and put his car in park and got out. He opened the passenger door and stopped me.

"What you mad at me for Journee I didn't do shit but keep it real with you?" He gritted his teeth and snarled.

"I'm not mad I kept it real with you too. If we going to the auction then I'll have my money."

"Alright smart ass I'll see you Friday. I'll be here by 3:30 pm don't be late and leave the attitude at the door." He laughed.

I didn't even respond. I felt him staring at me as I walked off. I walked in the house and locked the door. My momma was sitting on the couch waiting for me.

"Journee, you ain't grown you're just sixteen. Y'all two have a thing for each other and don't even know it. Are you having sex?" My mother asked.

"No mother I'm not having sex. I don't look at him like that."

"Well he is looking at you like that. I'm putting you on birth control Journee Leigh Armstrong. I'm not taking any chances in case you start looking at him like that." My mother stated.

"Mother are we really having this conversation?"

"Yes, we are Journee you think your grown. You are driving his car and fixing him plates of my food so yes we gone talk about it." My mother stated.

"I don't think I'm grown. I'm not messing with him. I only drove his car because he wanted to eat and he wanted me to ride up the block with him, while he dropped his money off that's it."

"Why did you take your bonnet off and why are your nipples are hard? I would say let me feel between your legs but I already know it's hot. You ain't looking him like that but your body language is. If you don't want him to get the wrong signal next time cover your body up if he's coming around." My mother stated.

"But Mother I tried to come back in the house and change clothes and he said I was fine."

"Of course, he would say that Journee he wanted to look at you. Did he let you get out the car?"

"No."

"That's exactly what I thought take you grown ass to bed take shower first. Good night I'm might be old Journee but baby your mother was the best to ever do it." My mother laughed.

"Good Night."

I took a shower was it that obvious. Juelz was cute I ain't gone lie but I never thought about him like that at all. I dried off and applied lotion my body. I checked my phone Nikki called me a few times and Juelz sent me a text.

Juelz- That ass getting fat you sure you ain't messing with nobody on the block.

I blushed because he was watching me. I was tempted to text him back but I didn't want our friendship to change. I left it alone. Juelz was very handsome I can't lie. He was perfect his caramel complexion, big brown eyes and he had the perfect set of lips that I wouldn't mind kissing and the goatee that adorned his face was always lined up to perfection.

Oh, and his body was right and covered with tattoos. He loved to take off his shirt and show off. He smelled so good Bond No.9 that's his favorite scent but I pushed that shit at the back of my mind every time because he was my boss and I was his employee. I didn't want to cross the line and complicate things, but I'm not focused on guys right now just these books and the paper that I was getting.

Juelz

Journee's a real piece of work. I know she got my text. I didn't realize she was that thick. What the fuck did I miss? Her breast was plump like balloons and her ass sat up like a stallion and it jiggled when she walked. I had to straighten my pants; her brown skin glistened like silk. I felt my dick get hard. I don't like being ignored at all. I couldn't stop thinking about her. I had to call her. Journee was going to be mine sooner than later she didn't know but she was.

"Umm hello." She answered sounding sexy.

"You didn't get my text message."

"I did Juelz but I didn't feel the need to respond because you need to stop looking at my ass when I walk off." She sassed and yawned.

"Journee, who was you waiting on to call? You tried to put your sexy voice on."

"Nobody Juelz I was sleep, unlike yourself I have to go to school in the morning. I don't have the luxury of trapping all night." She sassed.

"Who you letting get deep off in them guts? You done got thick Journee don't lie either."

"Juelz, you are not my man. Why do you assume that because I've picked up a few pounds, I'm having sex with someone? It's the cornbread and the cabbage. I'm still a virgin sex doesn't cross my mind. Good night jerk." She laughed and hung up the phone in my face.

I wanted to know because some nigga was about to come up missing. She wasn't mines yet but she was next in line to be. My only problem is Giselle ugh why won't she leave. I've been trying to break things off with her for a minute now but she's so caught up with other shit to realize what the fuck is going.

Chapter 3-Journee

Juelz had to be thinking about me, because I for damn sure wasn't thinking about him. There goes that ache between my legs. I know you got my text. I sure did and smiled all night thinking about him watching me. I can't lie Juelz is fine, too damn fine and he can have any girl that he wants but he's looking at me. I need to stop thinking about him and he needs to stop thinking about me.

***

I couldn't sleep for shit thinking about Juelz all damn night. I had to get up at 5:50am to cook breakfast for my brother and sister and my mom. I had to be at school by 7:15am. I made everybody omelets this morning. I was in a rush and this will have to do.

I didn't get any sleep. I had my uniform laid out already. White Polo shirt and a Polo Khaki skirt I took my hair down. It flowed down my back so pretty. I applied baby oil to my legs. I had some fresh white air max that I paired with my outfit.

I kissed my mother on her forehead. I left out the door and headed to school. I refused to be late. I placed my earbuds in my ear. It took me about fifteen minutes to walk to school. I didn't get to exercise as much as I wanted too. I considered my morning walks as exercise.

Juelz

I stayed at the trap last night. I didn't even go home. Giselle blew my phone up talking about what little young bitch was driving my car. She pulled up at the trap house tripping making my spot hot trying to argue and fight. I had to choke her dumb ass out and send her back home.

I got so many drugs up in here I'll catch a life sentence. I really stayed over here to catch Journee and take her to school. I'm running late Nikki said she leaves about 6:45am. It's 6:50am. I'm running late I might be able to catch her. I sped to her house.

I pulled up on her block. I saw her she was at the stop sign on the corner. I hit the horn to see if she would turn around she didn't she kept going. I through my car in my park and ran up on her. I put my arms around her waist she was still waiting at the stop sign. She turned around and gave me the meanest scowl.

"Let me take you to school."

"For what, I like to walk in the morning to get my mind right. Stop walking up on me." She argued and rolled her eyes.

"Well you ain't walking today. You need to take those earphones up out of your ear. You're not even paying attention to your surroundings."

"Juelz my daddy is dead. Don't tell me what to do." She argued.

"Journee get your little ugly ass in the car before I pick you up and carry you to the car."

"I'm not beat for your shit today Juelz ain't nobody told you to give me a ride to school. I walk every day and I'm cool with that." She argued and walked toward the car.

"Why are you so mean?"

"I'm not mean Juelz. I like walking to school in the morning. It helps me clear my mind. I have a lot of things going on in my life, this is the only time I can think and not worry about stuff. I need these fifteen minutes." She explained.

"Oh, ok I'm sorry I didn't know."

"You good," She stated.

"Who be trying to holla at you?"

"Nobody why?" She asked very irritated.

"I just asked I wanted to see was there any competition."

"Yeah whatever, since you're curious it's plenty of competition. I'm just not interested." She stated.

"Yeah whatever, get your little ugly ass up out of my car and take your ass to class. I'll see you later."

"Whatever Juelz with your ugly ass." She laughed and slammed my door.

I sent her a text telling her don't slam my door. She responded.

Journee- Whatever ugly.

Nikki

I don't know what the fuck Journee and Juelz got going on but baby Giselle came to trap last night tripping. I didn't even know he was fucking with this bitch like that. I know Ashley ran her mouth she used to fuck with Skeet. Giselle walked in with Ashley right behind her and I was sitting on Skeet lap.

I laughed in that hoe face because she was funny. Skeet was mad but I don't care. I wanted Ashley to get out of line because I was ready to bust that bitch in her face. Juelz likes Journee. Journee is green but not that green. I can already tell that her and Giselle will have some problems in the future. I'll ask her about that in lunch.

I need Journee to spill the tea because I'm thirsty. I noticed how Juelz was about to knock my head off because I asked her to step out of the car. I wanted the streets to talk. My best friend bagged the plug.

We can get this double dating shit popping. Giselle was pissed Juelz choked her dumb ass out, that's what the fuck she gets. Bitch this is a fucking trap house any minute the FEDS or the police can swarm this bitch because you walk up here in your feelings. Ashley looking all dumb and shit. I told that hoe fix your fucking eyes and get the fuck up out of here. Skeet knows my young ass don't play that bullshit. Dismiss this hoe before I do.

***

<u>Journee</u>

Ugh I couldn't even focus at school. I've been thinking about Juelz all day and how he walked up behind me on the corner this morning with his hands wrapped around my waist. I couldn't stop smiling; I was blushing hard as fuck. His breath up against my neck I felt that tingle between my legs again. I can't even eat lunch. Everybody was looking. I'm sure the streets were talking but I don't care because we ain't official.

"Damn Journee he got you gone." My best friend Nikki taunted me.

"Who?"

"You know who don't act. You got everybody talking." My best friend Nikki stated.

"Who Juelz? Girl stop oh that's why they are looking and giving me dirty stares. You know what it is Nikki. I work for him in case you forgot."

"Journee Leigh girl your hell, but you know I know you. You ain't got to lie to me. If you say that's its just work than that's what it is but from what I saw last night somebody wants it to be more. He ain't letting anybody whip that Benz." My friend Nikki explained.

"Nikki, you swear you know me. You stay at the trap house with Skeet that's what the fuck y'all got going on? Juelz and I don't have shit going on but this money we're getting but that's a wrap because my mom found out. I was just riding with him so we can drop off the package that's it."

"Damn for real Journee? Let's be honest you and everybody know what Nikki and Skeet got going on. What you gone do now?" My friend Nikki asked in a very concerned tone.

I could tell Nikki anything she would never put my business out in these streets she was the definition of a real friend.

"Well, Juelz has another job for me that don't include hustling. I'm going to be cleaning houses and cooking."

"That's what's up. How are you going to get to the houses?" My best friend Nikki asked.

"Juelz is taking me to the auction tomorrow to get a car."

"Damn Journee, you about to be whipping before me. I'm glad bitch and nobody better not be up front besides Khadijah or Ms. Julissa and you better not have your seat pushed up to the steering wheel." My best friend Nikki laughed.

"Girl bye I'll see you later."

* * * *

The bell finally rang school was out. I was tired. I didn't get any sleep last night. I cut my cell phone back on. I didn't have any homework. I was frying fish and potato wedges with coleslaw and hush puppies on the side for dinner tonight. After that I planned to take a shower and going straight to bed.

Tomorrow was Friday and I only had two classes thank God. I could go to the bank to get a cashier's check. I made it home at my normal time in about fifteen minutes. When I approached my house; I noticed Juelz car parked out front. What was he doing at my house? He's doing too much now. I stopped and looked inside of Juelz car he wasn't inside. I walked in my house because Juelz wasn't in his car. I wanted to know what he was doing here.

"Journee Leigh your friend Juelz stopped by to introduce himself. He's a nice guy and very handsome." My mother stated.

"Mother don't pump his head up, he's ugly and rude as they come. Are you ok?" I laughed.

"Stop Journee he's a nice guy. I invited him to have a dinner with us." My mother stated and winked her eye at me.

"Mother is you cooking? Last I checked I done the cooking around here and not you."

"Journee cut it out; you fix him plates of my food everyday anyway. What's the problem with him eating with us?" My mother asked.

"Nothing mother."

"Alright that's settled I'm going to my room. Juelz make yourself at home. Journee be nice, if she acts out

Juelz my room is on the right knock and let me know ok."
My mother stated.

Chapter 4- Juelz

I fucked Journee up with that one. I might as well get to know my mother in law. Her daughter was mine rather she knew it or not.

"What's up Juelz? Why are you here? Leave my mother alone please? She's already sick and I don't need her defending you." She sassed.

"What's up Journee calm down; I'm here because I want too. I just wanted to meet your mother is that ok? I'm sorry." I stated and raised my hands up. "Don't hurt me."

"Whatever Juelz." She stated and rolled her eyes.

Journee's mother was cool; she grilled the shit out of me. She wanted to know what my intentions are with her daughter. I told her that I liked Journee but with the age difference she was too young for me to pursue her. She wasn't buying that shit; she gave me a look like nigga you are lying.

Her mother is messy too she stated that Journee had a few guy friends but nothing too serious. My nostrils instantly flared up and she noticed. She laughed in my face and stated boy you better lock Journee down and stop using that age excuse before you have high blood pressure at an early age. I couldn't do anything but shake my head and rub my hands across my face.

Journee

What's really going on with Juelz? I'm a little shocked by my mother's whole approach. I wouldn't dwell on it right now. I walked toward my bedroom to change clothes. I took off my shirt and skirt off. I laid it on my bed. I heard a knock at the door.

"Come in."

"Damn you thick as fuck." He whispered.

"Juelz get out you're making me uncomfortable and you're going to get me in trouble." I whispered and tried to cover up and push him out of my room.

"Don't hide from me. Your perfect." He whispered.

"Juelz, you should not be in my room." I whispered.

"I just wanted to see your room. I didn't know you were undressing." He whispered.

"Whatever."

He walked up behind me and wrapped his arms around my waist. I removed his hands and he tried to stop me.

"I just wanted to see if we'll look good together but you ugly." He laughed.

"Like you cute. Get out."

What is really going? Did I miss something Juelz is flirting too hard? I'm scared to be around him alone; he might take my virginity. I threw on an oversized shirt and some shorts. I placed my bonnet on and headed back to the kitchen to prepare for dinner.

I couldn't even look at him. I cut both deep fryers on. I changed the grease out yesterday. I seasoned the fish with garlic. I cut onions and peppers up. I placed the hush puppies in the fryer first and next I would drop the fries and fish. I brought some coleslaw from Publix.

Khadir and Khadijah would be making it home any minute now. I can hear Khadijah's mouth now.

"Why are you quiet Journee?"

"I'm not I have to make sure my food is on point. I love fish, how many pieces do you want?"

"Two, you need some help? He asked.

"Juelz, you can't even cook. Thank you for offering."

"How do you know what I can and can't do?" He asked.

"You might can cook, but I don't like anybody helping me when I'm cooking."

I heard the door open that's must be Khadijah and Khadir.

"Journee what are you doing with this boy in the house? I'm telling Momma on you." My sister Khadijah ranted.

"Oh, Khadijah your mother knows he's here."

"Are you sure Journee? I don't believe momma would let you have your boyfriend over here and she's in her room. When will the food be ready? I'm starving." My sister Khadijah ranted.

"Khadijah he's not my boyfriend. Chill out you know it doesn't take that long for fish." If looks could kill I would beat the brown off Khadijah's ass right about now. She was embarrassing me in front of him.

"Khadir do you have any homework?" I knelt, and gave him a hug so I could be eye level with him.

"No Journee, I don't have any." My brother Khadir stated.

"Ok cool, grab your snack and change your clothes and your dinner will be ready in minute."

"He's your favorite huh?" He asked.

"I don't have a favorite."

Khadijah

It's not fair Journee gets to have a boyfriend and I don't. I marched into my mother's room to see what was going on.

"Mother I'm home."

I climbed in the bed with her.

"Hey, Khadijah, how was your day?" My mother asked and kissed me on my forehead.

"It was fine. I didn't know Journee was dating and had a boyfriend. Can I have one too?"

"Khadijah, you are too young for a boyfriend. Last I checked Journee wasn't dating and the guy in the living room that's not her boyfriend." My mother stated.

"Journee gets to do everything. That's not fair."

"Khadijah shut up and stop complaining. Unlike you Journee isn't focused on boys she focused on her books that's what the fuck you need to focus on. Do I make myself clear Khadijah?" My mother asked.

"Yes mother, are you sure that's not Journee's boyfriend?"

"Khadijah I'm very sure, I can assure you."

My mother was keeping something from me. I may be young but I'm not that dumb. Journee has never had a guy over before. When I walked to my mother's room. I stood in the hallway just to watch the two of them. I noticed him looking at Journee like she was piece of meat. Journee could fool my mother and everybody else but she couldn't fool me.

I'm going to ask Nikki she wouldn't hesitate to tell the truth. If Journee could have a boyfriend I could too. I don't care what my mother was talking about. I'm focused on my books enough.

Chapter 5-Journee

Finally, I finished cooking. My fish was fried and seasoned to perfection. The hush puppies smelled great and the steak fries were yummy. I made some green apple Kool-Aid last night, I couldn't wait to fill my cup. I couldn't wait to eat. My food was going to melt in my mouth. Literally I could taste the fish on my tongue.

I fixed everybody a plate. Juelz sat next to me. My mother said grace. Damn his cologne smelled so good none of that mattered right now. My plate that sat in front of me was about to be devoured.

Khadijah had an attitude all night. I couldn't wait to check her as soon as Juelz leaves. Khadijah's three years younger than me. I'm sure she had an attitude because Juelz was here. Khadijah wants a boyfriend so bad because all her friends have one. I love my sister to death but I refuse to let her be like her fast as friends.

***

Everybody finished dinner. Juelz and I cleaned the kitchen. We kept stealing glances at each other but we both ignored it.

His phone was blowing up but he didn't answer it. It annoyed me but I couldn't be mad because he wasn't my man. I was single and shouldn't be catching feelings. I need to check my damn self.

"I'm about slide up out of here you good?" He asked.

"I'm fine."

"All right I'll see you tomorrow. Walk me to my car." He asked.

I did as I was told. Juelz phone was still blowing up. I ignored it. We made it to his car.

"Damn is that you Journee? Your ass is fat than a motherfucker you done got thick as fuck. Let me take you out on a date." My childhood friend Juan yelled.

Oh, shit I could feel the heat radiating off Juelz.

"Juan shut the fuck up talking to me like that. You know better. Let me get Samantha's number and tell her you have a wondering eye." I laughed.

"Let me get up out here since your little boyfriend pulling up on his bike and shit." He laughed.

"Yeah whatever Juelz bye. Answer your phone so your little girlfriend can stop calling."

I walked off and headed back in the house. I threw my phone on the bed and headed to the shower. I'm confused I don't know what we are doing.

Juelz

I hate to admit, but Journee can throw down in the kitchen. Her mother was cool. I could tell that her sister was a handful, next time I would bring my brother Smoke with me he's fifteen around her sister's age.

I couldn't even enjoy the food like I wanted too because Giselle kept calling my mother fucking phone. I bet she hasn't cooked shit for dinner. I should've left her right where I found her on Jonesboro Rd. A long time ago. Giselle was only nineteen and she didn't want anything for herself but a nigga with some cash, nice cars, and bags that's it.

We've been together for about a year now. I regret that shit everyday too. One of the reasons I was attracted to Journee because she's everything that Giselle isn't. She takes care of a whole family and she's only sixteen. She's not your average sixteen-year-old. I like her but she's too young I'm nineteen.

<u>Giselle</u>

Juelz got me fucked up. I love him and I'm never letting him go. He's been acting strange. My cousin Ashley called me last night and stated that he had some young girl driving his Benz last night. I have never drove his Benz or any of his cars. We live together that's very disrespectful. I don't ask for much but respect.

I pulled up last night at the Trap house to see what's going on and who was driving his car. I threw my fighting clothes on and put Vaseline on my face. Everybody in Bankhead knew Juelz was my man and I staked claim to him. I had to check a few hoes here and there but I have never received a phone call about any females driving his car.

I couldn't believe how nonchalant he acted. He got aggressive with me and choked me out. Tears poured in my eyes just thinking about last night. He sent me home and he didn't even come home. To make matters worse Skeet's girlfriend or whatever she is Nikki had the nerve to laugh in my fucking face. What's funny about a woman getting choked by her boyfriend because she's concerned. Who is she? Let me call him to see if he's bringing his ass home tonight.

"Juelz are you coming home tonight?" I pouted.

"Maybe did you cook?" He asked.

"No, I ordered us something."

"I'll be there later don't wait up."

"Who is she?" I cried.

"It's just you Giselle it ain't no she it's you." He yelled, through the phone and hung up.

Nikki

Damn I should call my best friend. The streets are talking about her and Juelz. Journee is being very secretive about what the fuck is really going on. Skeet and I rode by her house and sure enough Juelz Benz was parked out front. I couldn't do anything but shake my head.

I would love to see Journee and Juelz together. I went home early tonight just so I could call Journee and see what's up fuck that I'm spending the night. I need details. Let me call my best friend.

"What Nikki, what do you want?" She answered with a fake attitude.

"I'm spending the night meet me at the stop sign that's what. Did you cook I'm high as fuck and I'm hungry?"

"Yeah I fried fish and steak fries and hush puppies. I brought some coleslaw from Publix." She stated.

"Journee why you didn't call me and tell me you fried fish? You know I love your fried fish plates."

"I honestly forgot. I got thrown off when I made it home." She laughed.

"Meet me at the stop sign. So, we can talk about how you got thrown off."

"Oh, so you're only coming to hang out with me to be nosy." She laughed.

"You damn right I am, don't act surprised I need to see your facial expressions. I need the motherfucking tea and I got some tea to spill."

"Bye Nikki I'm leaving out the door now." She laughed.

Journee met me at the stop sign. We walked back to her house. Khadijah texted me earlier being nosy about Journee and Juelz. I couldn't tell her anything because I didn't know anything.

Juelz

I've been with Giselle for about a year. I'm not in love with her but I tolerate her. She's spoiled as fuck and I feed her addiction. I want more for Giselle than she wants for herself. I like Journee I'm probably in love with her but I must figure out this thing out with Giselle and me.

I never seen her shed tears before and I don't want her crying behind me off assumptions. I'm going to take my ass home even though I don't want too. I need to bust a nut even though I don't want Giselle to get me off she'll have to do for now.

Giselle is crazy cutting her off would be harder than I think because she's too attached. Even though she knows things are not good with us she's not trying to change her ways. I couldn't make anybody change their ways. It was up to them to change and Giselle was content with her life.

I knew Ashley was the one running back telling her shit. That's just the type of female she is. I can't wait for Nikki to lay hands on her. Ashley met Skeet through me she begged me to hook her up with him. They weren't exclusive but they were kicking it somewhat.

Chapter 6-Journee

"What's up Nikki?" I smiled.

"Don't what's up me Journee Leigh." My best friend Nikki laughed.

We walked back to my house. Nikki was on the phone arguing with Skeet. I thought it was cute. We made it back to the house. I dropped Nikki two pieces of fresh fried fish and few fries. I buttered some bread and cut up a tomato and some lettuce and onions. Nikki loves to make a sandwich with her fish. I didn't want to hear her mouth.

"Look what the wind blew in. Hey, Nikki, how nice to see you. You haven't been by here to see me since you started selling drugs too." My mother laughed.

"Auntie Julissa, don't do me. We are better than that. I've been busy but I'm here today that's all that matters." My best friend Nikki stated with the biggest smile she could muster up.

"Umm huh tell me anything. Y'all two are too damn grown. I heard about you Nikki. Khadijah wants to be just like you and Journee she had the nerve to ask me could she have a boyfriend too. Hell no." My mother explained.

"Auntie Julissa you heard about me. It's a big deal when a Queen such as yourself has heard about little ole me." My best friend Nikki laughed.

"Hurry up Nikki and eat your damn food, so we can get the tea on Journee and Juelz. I'm listening carefully. I know he snuck in Journee's room earlier." My mother stated.

"Dang Journee you didn't tell me that." My best friend Nikki stated.

"Umm huh she likes him and she know that she does." My mother stated.

"Mother are you really sitting here talking about me to Nikki like I'm not here. Juelz is cool, I like him as a friend that's it, but when he came in my room. I let him know that he shouldn't be here. I respect your home and I know right from wrong." I hope I pulled that off well. Who am I kidding. I'm smitten with Juelz I like him a lot.

"Journee, you ain't that good at lying. I know you I'm your mother. I created you. The only reason I invited him to dinner is because I wanted to see how the two of y'all interacted with each other and I wanted to see if you'll be comfortable enough to talk about him with me." My mother explained.

"Mother what do you want me to say? I like him he's the finest nigga gracing the West Side. I love his caramel complexion his white teeth. Oh, and the six pack that adorns his stomach his lips umm their kissable. The tattoos that cover his body damn oops? The waves that are sculptured in his hair has every girl getting sea sick and he looks like God created himself, his swag is on one thousand. Yes, he's that nigga his pockets are on swollen and I'm feeling him."

"Yes, that's what fuck I wanted your hot ass to say. Keep your hot ass away from him, before he attempts to get in your panties." My mother laughed.

"Mother you tricked me." I laughed.

"No Journee, I kept it real with you. Always express your feelings and let someone know your true feelings for them you're human. It's also good to guard your heart too. I want you to live a little. I'm going to try to do a little more around the house. I want you to experience your teenage years. I'm going to bed. You and Nikki clean up my kitchen and take y'all asses to bed." My mother stated. She kissed me and Nikki on our forehead and went to bed.

Nikki

"Journee, the fish was really good. Auntie just read your ass she's cool as fuck she's a real OG I heard about auntie Julissa back in the day."

"Nikki shut up, go wash your funky ass smelling like Skeet. Hurry up so I can vent before I go to sleep and dream about Juelz." She laughed.

"You don't have to tell me twice. I like the new Journee."

I hopped in the shower to handle my hygiene. Skeet called my phone at least twenty times since I've been here. I made myself clear earlier. If Ashley isn't an issue, then why is she still hanging on the block. I told him if I catch that bitch up there tomorrow. I'm beating her ass. She's always staring at me. It's not about him. It's the principle quit looking at me and my nigga.

"Journee spill the tea. You like Juelz huh? He likes you too I know that for a fact. I can tell by the way he looks at you. Let me keep it real with you. He has a situation. I don't know if it's serious but this girl from the south side

Giselle Lawrence she's a dirty south hoe from Jonesboro. She's Ashley cousin that use to fuck with Skeet.

Word traveled fast about you driving his car that hoe pulled up with Vaseline all on her face ready to fight. I laughed in the hoe face she was furious. Journee, you know you are my bitch for life girl I was ready to beat her ass. Skeet had to hold me back. Juelz sent her on her way he choked her ass out.

What really triggered me was Ashley she was staring at Skeet the whole time. I was sitting on his lap bitch get the picture it's me and not you. I'm telling you now, me and that hoe gone have some problems. I told Skeet let me catch her on the block tomorrow and she keep looking at me. I'm beating her ass I'm not asking any questions. I'm running up and I'm going to Donkey Kong that hoe real shit."

"Nikki stop you damn fool. Oh, so ole girl was mad huh. It might be something because somebody kept blowing his phone up when he was over here. He's not my man. I'm tripping she was ready to fight Nikki Vaseline and all that's funny. Handle your business. I like Juelz I'm not gone lie but I don't have time for the drama." She stated.

"I'm just telling you because you are my best friend ain't no nigga or bitch gone play you that's just a heads up. If you like him and he likes you ain't nothing a bitch can do about it. Y'all can be friends. Move with caution. My phone started ringing. It was Skeet.

"What Skeet?"

"Come outside." He said.

"For what?"

"Damn I just want to see you. Tell Journee to call Juelz he's lonely." He laughed.

"Alright bye."

"Good night Nikki, go see what your man wants and hurry up before my nosey as mother wakes up." She stated.

"I am, Skeet said call Juelz he's lonely."

"Yeah whatever, I'm going to bed." She stated.

<u>Journee</u>

As usual I couldn't sleep last night thinking about Juelz. Nikki stayed on the phone all night talking to Skeet. Their relationship is so cute. I overslept I woke up at 6:20 am sleep finally consumed me at about 1:30 am.

I had to get dressed for school. My mom woke everybody up and made breakfast Sausage egg and cheese biscuits. It smelled so damn good. I thumbed through my closet to find something to wear. On Fridays, we could dress down of course I was getting clean. I opted out for a Calvin Klein maxi dress and blue jean jacket and some sandals.

I got my feet done last Saturday and I have yet to show off my pretty toes that were freshly painted white. I threw some flexi rods in my hair last night. I'm tired of flat ironing my hair. I jumped in the shower to handle my hygiene. I love the smell of this Dove body wash. I dried off. I brushed my teeth quick. Nikki was banging on my door talking about don't run all the hot water out. She should've kept her nosey ass at home.

I wrapped the towel around my body and I decided to get dressed in my room. I applied bath and body works Cucumber Melon lotion to my body. One of the neighborhood boosters stole me a whole bunch of Tommy Hilfiger bra and panties sets in every color. I put my dress on, applied some deodorant and grabbed my jacket. I took my hair down it was pretty.

"Don't you look cute." My mother stated.

"Thank you."

"Turn around let me see you from the back." My mother laughed.

I turned around and gave my mother a full spin. I couldn't help but smile because she was more excited than me about Juelz and me.

"Journee Leigh, you are filling out pretty nice. You got the dope boys going crazy." My mother laughed.

"Mother stop."

***

It was 6:45am it's was time for me to leave and walk to school. I was waiting on Nikki she just had to get another sausage egg and cheese biscuit. My mother gave her one to go. We started walking up the street toward the school.

Skeet and Juelz pulled up behind us in separate cars. Nikki already knew the deal her eyes and smile lit up she was glad to see her boo. She hopped in the car. I kept walking I already told Juelz yesterday I liked walking I needed these fifteen minutes. He tooted the horn and I threw my hand up and waved and kept walking. He called my phone. I answered after the second ring.

"Damn Journee a nigga drove all the way over here to take you to school. Get your ass in the car. I don't care about you needing fifteen minutes to get your mind right. If I have to get out the car. We are going to have some issues." He stated.

"Whatever Juelz bye."

I wonder why he thinks he can talk me like he's my daddy or my man. Last, I checked my father was dead and I'm single unless I'm missing something. I walked to the car and got in and slammed the door. I knew that pisses him off.

"Good Morning Juelz. How are you?"

"I'm good but I'll be better if you stop playing hard to get. You know I came to pick you up."

"No, I didn't know Juelz you didn't run that by me."

"It's getting hot so I assume you want to be grown and show my body off huh. You want niggas looking at you? I have never saw you wear a dress before but today you want to put this tight as dress on and walk to school and show off my body. You got me fucked up Journee." He yelled.

"Hold up Juelz back up, last I checked I was single so I'm confused. This body is mine and I wear dresses all the time. What would I need to wear a dress to the trap for? You are sending me mixed signals, let it be known what you are trying to do.

I heard about your little girlfriend coming to the trap with some Vaseline. Tell that duck to be easy, I don't bother anybody but she doesn't want any problems with me."

"You know I want your young ass you just wanted me to say it. I don't have a girlfriend and you won't have any issues."

' "I'm dating someone." I laughed.

"Journee, you think this shit is game. I asked you, was talking to somebody and you said no. Are you fucking him that's why all of sudden you so fucking thick and your ass is spreading? Tell me who in the fuck you are talking too." He yelled in my face.

"Bye Juelz I don't have time for this. This is the reason I like to walk to clear my mind and not filter it with your assumptions." I tried to unlock the door he had the child lock on. He sped off fast like a fucking maniac.

"You shit out of luck Journee, answer my fucking question before you think about going anywhere."

"Juelz, you gone make me late for school."

"Walking ain't gone get you there faster."

"I'm not dating anyone. I just wanted to mess with you." I whispered.

"Nah Journee, speak up. I can't fucking hear you. Repeat that shit." He gritted his teeth and snarled.

"If you can what, you can hear."

"Journee your young ass like playing with a nigga like me. You gone regret that shit. I make the fucking rules. You belong to me understand that shit and respect it." He explained.

"I belong to you since when? If you wanted to ask me out, then you need to come correct. You can't force me to be with you that shit ain't happening. I'm late for school. We can talk about this later."

"You heard what the fuck I said, I'll be here after your last class."

Oh God what have I gotten myself into. Juelz is crazy and too aggressive. When did we become a couple?

I'm confused. He's jealous he said that he and Giselle wasn't anything so I'll hold him to his word.

Chapter 7-Juelz

I tried to hold back but she took me there. I put myself out there. I want Journee it's not one nigga or bitch out here that can stop me from getting her. I wish they would. I lied to Journee and told her I wasn't with Giselle shit in my eyes I wasn't I laid my head there sometimes when she begged me too but I had three houses that she didn't know about at all.

I paid all the bills. Her crib was in her name. I had a few things over there but not much. I need to sit down with Giselle and explain to her what the fuck is going on because it ain't no us. We can continue to be friends and I'll help her whenever she needed help but I was tired of footing the bill on everything.

I'm young but I'm tired of running through chicks. I needed somebody that I could build with and Giselle didn't fit that description. She couldn't even boil rice she didn't want her own money she wanted mine. She wouldn't even bag pills or break down weed but as soon as we ran out and she heard me running the money through the money counter she would have her hand out.

Giselle

I should be happy but I'm not. Juelz does everything for me and I'm very thankful for that. I want Juelz to commit. He finally came home last night. I shouldn't have to beg him to come home if we are in a relationship.

We didn't make up, but I wanted him to make love to me but he didn't he just fucked me. He apologized but I felt in my heart that it wasn't genuine. I know it's somebody else I could feel it. He strapped up last night and he never does that.

I kept trying to kiss him but he wouldn't let me. I placed my hands on his chest and he smacked them off. I started crying and asked him what's wrong, what did I do. He wiped my tears and told me that I needed to grow up. I needed to do something for myself because he was about to stop taking care of me.

What the fuck did that supposed to mean? I graduated from High School but I didn't want to go to college. As far as I can see we're even he doesn't work he sells drugs Monday through Sunday. When he gets a real job so will I, but until then I'm not doing shit but shopping and relaxing. I thought about cooking him some breakfast but he was gone before I woke up. I called Ashley to see what she was up too.

"Hey cuddy what are you doing?"

"Nothing cooking Skeet some breakfast. I'm about to put this pussy on him while his little girlfriend at school what are you doing?" My cousin Ashley lied.

"Girl please tell me you are fucking lying?"

"No, I'm not we are still messing around. I just tolerate whatever him and Nikki got going on but he's always here when she's at school and when she goes home he's here too. Let me send you a picture. He ain't never left me. I think it's time I teach this little young bitch and Skeet a lesson.

"Ashley, what are you about to do?"

"The same shit your dumb ass needs to do. I'm letting Nikki know soon. You on my phone you need to be on Juelz line he's feeling Journee's young ass she's your replacement." My cousin Ashley stated.

"Can't no bitch replace me not even Journee whoever the fuck she is. Juelz lays his head here every night and what he does on his time isn't an issue because he's still breaking bread with me. I'm whipping a Lexus. I'm in a condominium that he furnished.

I have a Chanel bag with bands on demand. I smoke nothing but the best. My closet laced with nothing but designer. So, excuse me who doing what not my man but yours. I shouldn't have called your bitter ass." I hung up in her face. That picture never came through lying ass bitch.

**

That's the problem with females they so worried about your man and what he's doing they don't even have a man. Ashley doesn't even have her own spot or a car. She's still living with her mother. I couldn't deal I was through fucking with her. I didn't like the shots that she was throwing.

Juelz isn't a saint and I'm not either. I don't accept what he's doing. We all got secrets. Everything you do in the dark comes to the light. I will never let him be with another female freely. I'm not having that shit over my dead body I'll be the EX from hell.

Journee

I finished my two classes and sure enough as soon as I stepped out of the building Juelz was waiting on me. I opened the door and got inside of the car. He pulled off as soon as I got in.

"How was your day? Did you think about what I said?" He asked and grinned at me.

"How could I not? Why me though?"

"Why not you? Are you going to be my girl or not? You really don't have a choice saying no isn't an option." He stated.

"Why are you making it so hard for me? We barely even know each other. I don't know the first thing about being in a relationship Juelz."

"When you want something as bad as I want you. You don't stop until you get it. I like you I really do. I want to be your first and last everything." He explained.

"Why do you want me so bad? Out of all the girls around. You want me Journee Leigh why?"

"It's plenty reasons. I'm glad you're not like other girls. I want you to continue to be you, you're a diamond in the ruff. You have so much potential and your drive is crazy and you're only sixteen and I'm attracted to that. I want to help you do it all." He stated.

"I don't know what to say Juelz."

"Just say you'll be mine." He laughed.

"I'll be yours Juelz but don't try to play me I'm serious. Make sure you let ole girl know that's it's you and me. I'm serious."

"Journee it's me and you until the world blow. Giselle and I aren't together we haven't been in together in a long time but if she needs reassurance then I don't have a problem reminding her." He explained.

"I'll take your word for it. Actions speak louder than words don't have me out here looking like a fool."

"Journee Leigh, look at me. I would never do that." He stated, he grabbed my chin and made me look at him.

"I'm going to hold you to that. Your word is our bond."

"Where too?" He asked.

"I'm hungry, take me home so I can fix me something to eat. I need to go to the bank to get a cashier's check."

"How about I'll cook for you at my house? Who do you bank with and we can stop by their first?" He stated.

"Normally on Fridays I go straight home. Let me run going to your house by my mom first?"

"Ok cool I respect that." He stated.

"Mom, Juelz and I are going to the auction. Is it ok if I hang out at his house for few hours?"

"Journee it's cool but put Juelz on the phone. Juelz, I don't know what your intentions are with my daughter today. I hope they are good.

I know you like her and she likes you but please don't break her heart and attempt to get any pussy from her until she's ready ok. Do I make myself clear? Journee you're getting on birth control Monday. I don't trust you and this grown lil nigga." My mother stated.

I'm so embarrassed. She has no filter why does she assume I'm automatically going to give it up? I just looked out the window. Juelz grabbed my hand.

"You good Journee whenever you're ready we'll take it there but right now I'm not focused on that. I want more than sex from you." He explained.

I nodded my head and enjoyed the ride.

Juelz

Ms. Julissa was crazy as fuck hell nah she went in. I wanted Journee but I wasn't going to pressure her for sex just yet. Sex wasn't going to stop me from kissing her and sucking on her and eating her pussy but when she's ready she'll let me know.

I had plans to buy Journee a car anyway but since she agreed to be my girl it's only right I purchase her a set of wheels.

"Juelz, you rode right past the bank." She yelled.

"Chill out I'm hungry we can come back to the bank later. We got plenty of time."

Journee don't miss a beat. I already know she's going to trip because I'm buying her car. Oh well she'll just be mad at me. I'll make it up to her.

***

We made it to my house out in Mableton in about thirty minutes. I opened the car door for Journee and escorted her in. I couldn't stop looking at her from the back.

Journee is built like Trina that's another reason I didn't want her walking to school because niggas be out here lurking.

I didn't want a nigga looking at nothing that belonged to me. Journee is innocent and a little naïve to some shit but a nigga will take her kindness for her weakness. I pay attention to all my surroundings. I noticed when I pulled up on her block. Every nigga on the corner was lusting behind her.

"Have a seat."

"Juelz what are you doing with this big house and it's just you?" She asked.

"Journee it's not that big. It's our house for when I wife you and you have my kids."

"Juelz you're full a shit, you talk a good game. You got plans for me, don't you?" She asked.

"I sure do, get comfortable take your shoes off."

"What are you cooking Juelz?"

"Hamburgers and Fries."

"Let me cook them. I like my burgers a certain way."

"Dang Journee why can't I cook for you? I know you can cook but I got this."

I walked up on Journee. I wrapped my arms around her waist.

"I got you trust me ok."

"Ok." She pouted.

Journee young ass gone fuck around and get this dick sooner than she think. Looking at me with fuck faces.

"Let me let you go so I can eat and take a nap."

"Yeah you do that. Which one is your room?" She asked.

"All of them."

"Whatever wake me up when the food is ready. I'm going to take a nap."

Journee offered to cook for us. Giselle would never do that. Journee made sure I ate good everyday that's one of the reasons that I was attracted to her. She kept a nigga fed. I didn't have to spend money eating out every day. I had a conversation with my mom about Journee and Giselle.

My mom said that Journee was a keeper and Giselle was a skeezer. My mom still lives in Florida. I moved out here with my dad and his new wife five years ago. I went to Florida every summer to see my mother and grandmother.

Chapter 8-Journee

Juelz had a nice house. I thought it was cute that he wanted to cook for me. I'm tired I needed a nap. I didn't get any sleep thinking about his ass last night. I found a room and took off my clothes. I found a shirt in the drawer and laid down. I was tired as shit. Lately I couldn't keep him off my mind since he started flirting with me. I didn't think that we would be in a relationship so soon.

He was determined and I like that about him. I would take it one day at a time. I'm curious to taste these hamburgers and fries. I'm hungry too. I'm still tripping off my mother she was so damn extra it didn't make no sense. She embarrassed the fuck out of me. Juelz just shook his head. My mother got straight to the point about everything she never beats around the bush. Khadijah is the same way.

I hate to face her when I get home. She'll ask me twenty-one questions. I know she's over protective because she had me young but I'm not interested in having sex yet.

Juelz

I went to check on Journee she was laid out on my bed with my shirt on. Her pussy was playing peek a boo. I climbed on top of Journee and kissed her lips, they were soft as fuck too. "Wake up Journee it's time to eat."

"Stop Juelz, I'm tired." She stated as she stirred in her sleep.

"Come on Journee wake up so you can eat. I want to take a nap also. We can lay down together. Take your shirt off so you won't get food on it." I bit her stomach.

"Whatever Juelz." She stated.

I had Journee's plate fixed already cheeseburger and fries. We sat down and ate.

"Juelz this is really good." She spoke with her mouth full.

"I know Journee, I can cook too."

"I was about to say something smart but I'll keep it to myself." She said under her breath.

We finished eating Journee washed the dishes. I put a movie on. She climbed in the bed with nothing on but her bra and panties and my shirt. I put so many hickeys on her neck it was ridiculous. She didn't object. We played around a little bit until we both got tired and went to sleep.

***

Journee and I woke up from our nap. To be honest this is the best sleep that I've had in a long time. I haven't slept in days. I don't even sleep this good when I crash at Giselle's. The auction ADESA Atlanta started at 4:00pm. It was a little after 3:00pm.

I wanted to get there a little early to look around. My uncle is a mechanic. I've been checking out the run list for a few days. I saw a few cars and SUV's that I wanted Journee to get.

I had my eye on a Mercedes truck. I knew Journee would trip about me getting it. It's a little too flashy for a sixteen-year-old but she'll be seventeen next couple of months. When Journee pulls up I want everybody to know that she's mine. Her license plate is going to say JUELZ.

"Wake up Journee so we can get to the auction."

"Juelz, we didn't go buy the bank. I guess I'll swipe my card my daily limit for purchases is three thousand. I'll call the bank to see if I can get my daily limit increased." She yawned while she spoke.

"Shut up Journee and come on. You are talking too damn much. Go brush your teeth and wash your face. You have a slobber on your face."

"Whatever." She laughed.

We put our clothes back on. I drove to the auction.

Journee

My mother is going to kill me. Juelz tore my neck up. His kisses had me going crazy. It felt so good laying in his bed. I know we would be having sex soon. I'm not going to lie first thing Monday morning I will be getting on birth control.

He climbed on top of me and started kissing me when I was sleep my panties were soaked. I threw them in the trash. I'm so embarrassed. I'm ready to get my first set of wheels. Khadijah sent me a text asking where I was. I told her that I was getting a car and I would be home as soon as I'm finished.

***

We finally made it to the auction. It was really packed. We could barely move. I think we may have been the youngest people here. I saw a few cars that I wanted but Juelz didn't like any of them. At this point I was getting pissed. It was my car anyway I don't see why he cared so much.

"Look Journee, I'm copping that Mercedes truck for you. You're my girl so you should ride a certain way. You're a reflection of me." He stated.

"Juelz that's too fancy. I'm good."

"Journee get you use to fancy shit. It ain't no turning back. I'm authentic." He boasted.

"That's all of my money." I pouted.

"Put your money up I'm buying." He stated.

"Juelz, I can't accept a Mercedes Benz from you?"

"Why, you said you was my girl right, why not?" He gritted his teeth and raised his voice.

"Yes."

"I want to spoil you Journee. Can I do that? I'm young fly a nigga with major paper and I want to blow a few bands on you. You are more than worth it. I know you ain't with me because I got it. I got us, I grind for us." He revealed.

Juelz purchased me a 2007 Mercedes-Benz M-Class SUV at the auction. It was nice as fuck. Leather interior the dashboard was wood grain.

He paid $17,000 for it including tags and title. He had my tags customized Juelz. He wanted everybody to know I was his. I guess he was serious about us being in a relationship. This truck sealed the deal.

I can only imagine how much the insurance would be a month. This is a luxury vehicle and I'm only sixteen. My mom would have to add me to her insurance.

"Journee, I added it to my insurance. Follow me to the car wash. I need to get the truck washed and detailed." He stated.

***

<u>Nikki</u>

Everything was cool with me and Skeet. I was chilling at the Trap and Ashley knocked on the door and asked for Skeet. She was surprised to see me. I told that hoe Skeet ain't here and slammed the door in her face. I didn't go to school today because I didn't feel good.

The hoe knocked on the door again. I looked through the peephole it was her. See this bitch is trying me. Let me call Journee and see where she's at because if I step outside I'm beating some sense into that hoe.

"Journee where you at?"

"Leaving my OBGYN why?" she asked.

"What's wrong?"

"I'm getting on the birth control shot." She stated.

"You and Juelz had sex already?"

"No not yet but you know how my mom is." She pouted.

"Come to trap ASAP Ashley with the shit and it's about four of them hoes outside. Journee, I swear to God I'm going to fuck this bitch up she just sent this picture of her and Skeet to my phone.

Hurry up and get here. Put that bat in your trunk. Do you have a crowbar? I'm about spas the fuck out, you know how I am. You're the only one that can calm me down."

"Nikki chill out I'm on my way. Don't go outside until I pull up because if a bitch put they hands on you and attempt to gang you while I'm not around. I'm clearing everything moving on Simpson Rd. I put it on my daddy. Give me twenty minutes. I'm on my way." My best friend Journee explained.

See that's why Journee Leigh is my best friend. Don't let that schoolgirl look fool you. My bestie doesn't play any fucking games or ask questions. She's on her fucking way. I wasn't even about to call Skeet. I wanted to beat Ashley's ass for a few months now but today was the mother fucking day. She got me all the way fucked up.

That's the problem with these old hoes from way back, they think because a bitch young and fucking with an older nigga they dumb and naive. Nah Not Nikki it's time I school her she's sending these old as pictures of her and Skeet to my phone. I got so much pressure built up. I'm going to do her so dirty, I dare a bitch to jump in she's going to regret fucking with me about my baby daddy Skeet. Yes, I'm pregnant that's why I'm sick.

***

Chapter 9-Journee

Nikki just found out that she was pregnant. She's making me auntie already Ashley got my girl fucked up though. She knew I was on my way. Ugh I hope I don't have to ever deal with bitter exes.

I made it on Simpson Rd. exactly in twenty minutes. As soon as I hit the block everybody was looking. I already knew why but I didn't even care. I saw Ashley posted up with a couple of bitches. She was looking hard to see who was getting out of the Benz. Juelz had my windows tinted Saturday.

I'm glad because these bitches are too nosey and I don't fuck with them. I duck them like these niggas do. I knocked on the door Nikki let me in.

"Look bitch this is how we are going to play it. We are not about to fight in front of the trap house because twelve will swarm the house and take everything up in here and that's my man and your man's money.

We are going to walk to the corner store and if her mouth gets reckless. You already know what time it is. Here's the bat and the crowbar which one are you working with?"

"Give me the fucking bat. Hold up Journee so you and Juelz are together?" My best friend Nikki asked.

"Yes, we are."

"No wonder you're pushing a Mercedes Benz truck at sixteen. I'm telling Skeet today I'm leaving his ass if he doesn't cop me a Benz or an BMW X5 and I'm carrying his first child." My best friend Nikki revealed.

"Nikki, I didn't even want Juelz to buy me a Benz because it's too flashy and I'm too young to be driving this. I wanted a Maxima or Camry."

"Damn Journee he brought the truck to?" My best friend Nikki asked.

"Yes, and I didn't want him too we kept going back and forth about it. I couldn't stop him he was determined."

"What Auntie Julissa say?" My best friend Nikki asked.

"I better get my ass on birth control because she already sees where this is going and she knows he's going to be my first and she's to fly to be a grandmother."

"Girl, Auntie Julissa knows a few things. I dreaded telling my mother." My best friend Nikki stated.

"It'll be all right. You're going to be a great mom. I can only imagine. My Godmother Valerie couldn't wait to blow my cover about not buying me shit and giving me money." I laughed.

"She sure couldn't." My best friend Nikki laughed.

We finished chopping it up for a few. Nikki put her clothes on. I stopped by the house and changed before I pulled up. I put my sweatpants on and t-shirt. When Nikki's mind is set ain't no changing it. So, we walked up the block and Ashley and her little friends were posted. Nikki and I were laughing because these bitches were funny.

"Aye Nikki did you like my picture? Every time you take your young ass to school our man can't get enough of me." Skeet's ex Ashley laughed.

I looked at Nikki and she looked me. I already knew what that meant.

"Keep walking Nikki let her approach you first she's begging for attention. Follow my lead if she runs up do that bitch dirty in the worst way. You already got the bat. Let's just see if she's dumb enough to keep picking."

We stood at the corner store for a few minutes. I grabbed me a jungle juice and a Little Debbie cake. Ashley and her crew walked up the block. It was fucking show time. I nudged Nikki she looked me. Everybody was out to all the dope boys were getting their car washed at the store. Niggas was shooting dice in the back. The old folks were playing the Cash 3 for the mid-day.

Nikki

It was going down on the corner everybody and they mammy was out. The dope boys trying to holler. Bitches looking for the next fuck. Crackheads looking for dope and I ain't gone none on me, but none of that shit matter to me.

I don't bother anybody, I only deal with two females Journee and Khadijah that's it. I'm not messy but on a good day fuck with me and I can be petty motherfucking Betty and today was the day.

Skeet called my phone I had to play it cool because if he had a clue I was about to beat Ashley's ass he would pull up and intervene. He was handling business with Juelz so I would see him later.

Ashley was still being loud and obnoxious I heard her mention my name. I tapped Journee and we started walking toward that way.

"That little young bitch doesn't want any with me." Skeet's ex Ashley laughed.

I don't know why she said that. I love Skeet and I'm crazy off the D. I dropped my purse on the ground. I swung the bat and busted that bitch dead in her fucking head.

You heard a loud thud. Once the bat knocked her in a daze. I picked that bitch up and slammed her in the concrete. We had a crowd now. The block was crazy. The dope boys stop shooting dice in the back because they heard it was a fight in the front.

All you heard was damn Nikki oh shit you giving that bitch the business. I was giving this bitch my best work. One of her home girls jumped in and Journee pulled that bitch up off me. Next thing I know Journee and that hoe started fighting.

Journee was giving that bitch her best work. Next thing we know the other two hoes jumped in. We really turned this mother fucker out then. I grabbed the bat. I started swinging wild as fuck knocking them hoes up off me and my bestie.

I beat Ashley so fucking bad they called the police. She was laid unconscious on the pavement. My nigga Jody said throw some water on that hoe she thirsty and she just got knocked the fuck out. I heard sirens. Somebody called twelve and we cleared it. Skeet and Juelz pulled down us as we were running back to the house.

"Nikki why in the fuck is you out here fighting and you pregnant with my seed." He yelled.

"Oh shit." I said under my breath.

Skeet

I'm so fucking pissed. I told Ashley's dumb ass to leave me the fuck alone. I got a girl and I'm good but no she wanted to be messy and keep fucking with Nikki and now she's in intensive care. Nikki is going to make me put my hands on her too.

I told her to chill out. I knew she was up to something because she rushed me off the phone. Lonzo just called my fucking phone and told me that Nikki and Journee was fighting up on Hollywood at the corner store with Ashley and her friends.

I just talked to Nikki and she said everything was good her and Journee walked to the store. Juelz and I just left this spot on Godby Rd. we're about to set up shop out there. I'm running stop signs and red lights and some more shit to see what's going on.

Lonzo said she shouldn't be fighting and she pregnant. His words blew me. I asked him who was pregnant and he said Nikki, she left her purse on the corner and her pregnancy test fell out it was positive.

Nikki already knows that I don't want her fighting and she's pregnant with my seed she got some fucking explaining to do. I'm not mad that she's pregnant. When the fuck was she going to tell me. I'm mad that's she's fighting and giving Ashley the benefit of the doubt.

To make matters worse she jumped in the car with Journee and they sped off after they got caught doing that hot ass shit on the corner. I called her phone and she cut it off. I guess she didn't want to talk but that wasn't an option.

Juelz called Journee and she said they were at her crib so we were about to pull up.

"Damn Skeet, Nikki got you gone and she pregnant. It's time to wife her." My right-hand man Juelz stated.

"Juelz I'm only nineteen and Nikki is seventeen I'm not thinking marrying nobody right now but this fucking paper."

"I'm just saying." My right-hand man Juelz stated.

Chapter 10-Nikki

I couldn't even deal with Skeet right now. As soon as he pulled down on us. I jumped in the truck with Journee and we pulled off. I didn't want to hear his mouth. I left my purse on the corner. Ebony sent me a text and said Lonzo grabbed my purse and gave it to Skeet.

It makes since now how he knows that I'm pregnant. I cut my phone off after that. Ashley wouldn't have gotten her ass beat if he would've checked the hoe a long time ago but no he was brushing that shit off.

This is what happens when I have to check a bitch. This is how I'm coming every time. I'm not sparing a hoe period. I don't care. Journee and I laid in her bed and laughed about this shit.

"What y'all two up too? I heard about y'all on the corner fighting. Don't run to my house after y'all done got the block hot." My Auntie Julissa asked.

"Auntie what don't you hear gosh." I laughed.

"I hear everything. Valerie told me your ass was pregnant. Umm huh y'all two are driving me crazy. You pregnant, Nikki you don't even know how to fuck properly. Journee probably next Juelz can't wait to break her off.

She's pushing a damn Benz at sixteen with custom plates this is too damn much. Khadijah grown ass wants a boyfriend. Where did y'all meet these grown niggas at any damn way?" My Auntie Julissa stated.

"I met Skeet at a basketball game when Westlake played Doug he almost ran me over when I was crossing the street. We exchanged numbers and the rest was history. I introduced Journee to Juelz. Auntie Julissa I'm about to piss myself you're too funny. Did you forget that Journee was in the room?"

"How could I not? That's the problem Nikki you and Journee was just pissing on y'all self a few years ago. Now y'all grown as fuck with boyfriends, selling drugs, fighting on the corner." My Auntie Julissa laughed.

"Hold up Auntie I wasn't pissing on myself a few years ago." I laughed.

"Nikki shut the hell up you know what I'm trying to say." My Auntie Julissa laughed.

"Journee get your mother please before I have a heart attack from laughing to death."

"Journee can't get me. Last, I checked this was my house and she's just an occupant. You two should get those niggas that just pulled up out front. Don't look scared now Ms. Fly at the mouth Nikki looking like Valerie in the face ass." My Auntie Julissa laughed.

My auntie is hell I swear if she mentions anything to Skeet and Juelz about me and Journee pissing on ourselves. I'm done.

Skeet

Journee stayed off Collier Rd. Me and Juelz pulled up. I haven't had a chance to really check out Journee's truck but damn Juelz got her riding nice. All hell is going to break loose once Giselle finds out. I should buy Nikki something now because I can already hear her mouth and she's pregnant. I'll never hear the end of that.

"Damn Juelz you sure you ain't trying to marry Journee she's riding real nice. What about Giselle?"

"I wouldn't mind. What about Giselle I'm not with her I'm with Journee and she's in a league of her own. Giselle isn't a factor. I don't care what she hears from the streets." My right-hand man Juelz stated.

"Yeah ok, well we at you girl's house go knock on the door and tell them to come outside."

"Hell, no you go do it." My right-hand man Juelz laughed.

"Man, is Journee momma crazy or something. I don't like knocking on nobody door who bat shit crazy.

"Skeet chill out man. She's like the older version of Nikki but worse." My right-hand man Juelz laughed.

"Oh hell no. You're trying to set me up for the kill. Come on let's get out of the car."

We walked up on the porch. I rang the doorbell. Journee's mother came to the door.

"Hey Juelz! Who is the grown lil nigga you brought with you? You must be Skeet. I heard about you too. You like going around getting young girls like Nikki pregnant. Get your lil knucklehead ass in my house now getting my damn niece pregnant.

Juelz who in the fuck told you to buy Journee a Benz truck. I'm telling you now if one of the duck as broads even think about fucking with mine. I'm beating ass I fight kids too. Journee and Nikki get y'all grown pissy asses in here." Journee's mother Ms. Julissa stated.

Journee momma was crazy as hell. I couldn't stop laughing she checked me and Juelz and then she checked Journee and Nikki and called them pissy. Juelz set me up but Journee's mom was cool as fuck. She was funny she had Nikki mad as hell checking her.

The next time she pisses me off I'm going to put Ms. Julissa on her. Nikki's mom was cool too. Ashley knew better I told her to leave me the fuck alone numerous of times but no she refused too.

I knew Nikki was crazy but she didn't believe me now she's fighting for her life because she couldn't let go.

Nikki

"Auntie Julissa, stop you're embarrassing us. Don't do me. I done told you ain't nothing pissy about me." I laughed.

See Skeet shouldn't have brought his ass down here because Auntie Julissa is crazy and she doesn't care what comes out of her mouth. Khadijah is the same damn way they haven't seen anything yet. Skeet and I locked eyes with each other.

"What's up?"

"You. Let's go outside so I can holler at you." My boyfriend Skeet stated.

We walked outside to his car. We locked eyes with each other.

"You pregnant with my seed? When were you going to tell me?" He asked.

"Yes, I'm pregnant with your child. I was going to tell you when you came back."

"Give me a hug. If something would've happened to you and my baby she would've been dead. I promise you.

Are you ok? What happened? I don't want you out here fighting no trash period." He stated.

"I'm fine Skeet. She knocked on the door asking for you. I told her you weren't here. She started talking shit about when I leave she's here and she sent an old ass picture of you and her to my phone. We fought up the street because I didn't want to get the Trap house hot with her foolishness."

"You did right. I don't want you on the block no more or at the trap period. I'm going to get us spot and get you a car this week. No more chilling up on Simpson period."

"I want a BMW X5 cocaine white customized plates NIK N SKT."

"Chill out, go get your stuff so we can go. Tell Juelz to get Journee to drop him off you hungry?" He stated.

"Alright I want Ruth Chris."

Juelz

"Journee, don't try to look and act like you're innocent. You were on the corner fighting too. Why did you pull off when we pulled up on you? I'm surprised I would've never thought you would be doing some hot as shit. Explain to me why the fuck you're fighting like a hood chick."

"Juelz, in case you forgot. I'm from the hood Bankhead Zone1, born and raised Collier St. I never said I was innocent. They tried to gang Nikki so I pulled one chick off her and she started popping slick at the mouth so it was on from there." She argued.

"What if you would've got locked up?"

"I didn't think about that." She argued.

"Next time think before you do shit. Going to jail and juvenile is always a possibility. Oh, ok keep your ass off the block too. Don't come up on Simpson Rd. unless I tell you too. Why didn't you go to school today?"

"I went to get on birth control is that ok with you? Juelz my daddy died a long time ago. I don't need you telling me what I can and can't do" She sassed.

"Why did you get on birth control? Are you having sex?"

"Juelz, I didn't want too but for the sake of my mother's sanity I had too. In case I decide to have sex." She stated.

"Journee, I don't want you taking that stuff. Whatever happens it just happens. I'm man enough to take care of anything I reproduce."

"I hear you Juelz trust me I do but I'm not ready for any kids. I don't want to be a teenage mother. I have enough of responsibilities of my own and a child doesn't fit the equation."

"I hear you Laila Ali, take me to my car please. Can I get a ride?"

"You sure can let me tell my mother where I'm going and I'll be right back." She argued and sassed.

"Lose the attitude I didn't do shit to you. I just told you how I felt."

Nikki

Skeet took that better than I expected. I was having his first child. It's only right. I'll be eighteen soon, and I graduate next month. My mom couldn't be too mad about me moving out. Ebony sent me a text stating that Ashley was in ICU and it wasn't looking so good. Ask me do I give a fuck? Ashley asked for everything that I gave her.

I was making statement for any bitch that wanted to try me behind Skeet that's how I was coming every fucking time. I'm paralyzing bitch's behind him. She tried me one too many fucking times. Today was the final straw.

I hate that Journee and Juelz is beefing behind this little shit, but that's my best friend more like my sister. Of course, she was going to have my back. Journee could fight too they didn't want no smoke with us.

"I meant what the fuck I said too. You did way too fucking much today." He yelled.

"I hear you Skeet but that was minor if the bitch ain't dead than I didn't do enough."

"You crazy as fuck Nikki." He laughed.

"You knew that already though, what's new. I'm crazy about that work you got between your legs." I smiled and grabbed his dick. He looked at me and smiled. Anytime he looked at me I couldn't do shit but smile. Skeet was everything to me.

"I'm not giving you no more. You're on punishment." He laughed.

"I wish you would try me like that."

Ashley was disrespectful she couldn't be grown enough and move on. She thought because I was young that she could fuck with me and it's not any consequences. I understood that y'all had some type of relationship but it's not what we have. It's no comparison.

Skeet felt he didn't need to check her. I knew she needed to be checked. Some niggas like bitches lusting behind them. I set the bar today. I don't play that shit. I'm not sparing a female. It's not even about Skeet. It's about my respect and willing to die for mine. You gone respect me.

Chapter 11-Journee

I can't believe Juelz chastised me like he did. We didn't even start the fight, we just finished it. My father is dead and last, I checked Julissa wasn't looking for a replacement. I know he could see the attitude all over my face. Nikki sent me a text stating that Skeet didn't even go off on her. He's buying her car and they're getting a place together.

I couldn't do anything but shake my head. Juelz has barely been my man for seventy-two hours and he thinks that he's running shit.

"Where to?"

"Mableton." He stated.

We drove in silence. I turned the radio up. I didn't have time for Juelz and his attitude. I made it to his house in about twenty-five minutes. I could feel him staring at me the whole time I was driving. When I finally pulled in his driveway and he noticed that I wasn't getting out of the car. He grabbed my keys out of the engine and told me to come in the house.

See this is the type of shit that I don't have time for. I don't want to argue the only thing that I want to do is lay down and get ready for school tomorrow and read a book normal shit.

"What's up Juelz?"

"Oh, you can talk now?" He yelled.

"What's wrong with you Juelz what did I do wrong?"

"Come sit on my lap Journee so daddy can tell you what you did wrong since you have no clue." He stated and motioned with his hands for me to come here.

"Why do I have to sit on your lap?"

"Because I want you to feel me that's why, do you have a problem with that?" He asked.

I did as I was told. I placed my purse on the couch and walked over to Juelz and sat on his lap. He started massaging my breast and biting me on my neck. He unsnapped my bra and freed my breast. I moaned so loud, it felt good.

"You like that Journee." He asked.

"It feels good."

"Let me stop I just wanted to relax you a little bit. I can tell you're very tense. I care about you and I'm sorry for snapping on you earlier. I don't want you out here fighting with these hood rats. I don't want that for you. I understand that you had to help Nikki but I don't want you caught up in the drama period do you understand me." He asked.

"I do, trust me Nikki didn't start the fight. Ashley wanted to fight at the trap house but I made sure we took that shit up the street."

"Good, I'm glad you were thinking. Another question. Birth control is cool but what if I wanted you to have my baby? If we have sex I wouldn't bust off in you off the rip but eventually I would. I don't like that birth control shit let nature take its course and if it happens it happens." He explained.

"Juelz, you already know how my mother is. She trusts me but she doesn't trust you so to ease her mind I had to get on birth control she wasn't haven't it, but I have to get home and get ready for school tomorrow and cook dinner."

"I'm hungry too can you feed me before you leave that is part of your new job you know?" He asked.

"Juelz, it has to be quick."

"That's fine meet me in my room while I get the stuff." He stated.

"Your room that's not the kitchen?"

"Journee shut up and do what the fuck I say to?" He yelled.

I rolled my eyes at him and made my way to his room. Juelz is going to fuck around and get me in trouble.

"Fix your eyes." He yelled.

I stood by the dresser waiting on Juelz to come back to his room. It was only a little after 4:00pm I figured I could make it home by 6pm if there's no traffic and have dinner ready before eight.

"Undress waist down." He smiled and yelled and licked his lips.

"Juelz I'm not doing this today. I'm not ready."

"Journee you're not doing anything. I want you to feed me. I want to eat you it's just oral sex." He stated. Juelz picked me up and threw me on his bed. He took my jeans off and tore my panties off with his teeth. I was so nervous.

Juelz propped my legs over his shoulders. He sprayed whip cream on my opening. He stuck his tongue deep off inside of me. He was slurping on me at very fast pace I'm sure the echoes could be heard throughout the house. The cover underneath me was soak and wet and my legs were shaking.

"Fuck my mouth Journee." He stated, it was muffled because he still had head between my legs. He grabbed my ass with his two hands and forced me to ride his face. I rode his face like I was horseback riding. I felt my knees buckle and I squeezed my toes tight. I guess Juelz could feel me tense up.

"Let that shit go cum for daddy." He yelled.

I let go and fluids started gushing out of me. I could feel it.

"Journee, you taste really good. Go clean yourself up and take your ass home." He licked his lips and laughed.

"No, I need to take a nap for a few. Wake me up at 5:00pm.

"Oh, so now you want to stay and take a nap since I sucked the soul out of your lil virgin pussy." He laughed.

"I sure do."

I got up and took a quick shower and dried off. Juelz was fast asleep I made it back to the bedroom and laid beside him.

***

I was so tired I overslept Juelz arms was wrapped around me so tight. It was 7:00pm. My mother was going to kill me. I had ten missed calls from her and two from Khadijah. I laid out the ground beef earlier to make hamburgers and fries that still wouldn't take too long.

I would tell her that I had to work technically I did work today. I had to feed Juelz. I'm going to get Khadijah more involved in the kitchen so she could learn how to cook also incase I'm not home she'll know what do.

"Juelz I'm about to leave." He was still sleep I kissed him on lips and as soon as my lips touched his. He shoved his tongue down my throat and wrapped his arms around my waist.

"You are leaving me baby?"

"Yep I already overslept I was tired but I needed the rest."

"Alright baby I'll see you later let me walk you to your car. Call me when you make it and I'll see you tomorrow." He stated and kissed me on my forehead.

I backed out of Juelz driveway and headed home. I connected the Bluetooth and decided to call my mother back to make sure that everything was ok. She answered on the first ring.

"Journee Leigh Armstrong where in the fuck have you been. I've called you at least ten times. I knew you took Juelz home but you never came back. You ain't grown." My mother yelled.

"I'm sorry mother we watched a movie and I fell asleep. I was supposed to leave at 5:00pm but I didn't hear my alarm."

"What else did you do besides watch a movie that has you so tired?" My mother asked.

"Nothing mother remember we had a fight earlier I was tired from that."

"Journee Leigh hurry up and get your ass home, so I can look you in your face to determine if you're bullshitting me." My mother laughed.

Julissa

I love Journee she is my heart, my first born but she isn't a good liar. That's perfectly fine with me and I wouldn't have it any other way. I want Journee to be comfortable to talk to me about what's going on in her life.

Her father was the same way he couldn't lie for shit. Journee and Juelz remind me of Julian and me when we were younger. She was tired. Tired of what if she gave him some of her pussy today. I'm going the fuck off.

I called her phone ten times too, she got some explaining to do. I cooked the hamburgers and fries and straightened up the house. Journee really didn't have to do as much of the stuff that she did around here. I think she likes the responsibility and to be in control of things.

***

Journee finally made it home it was a little after 7:30pm she was strolling through the door. She placed her purse on the couch. Watch this.

"Journee come here and give your mother a hug." She did as she was told.

"Follow me to my room. I cooked the hamburgers already I'll drop you some fresh fries when I finish talking to you."

"You cooked already mother." My daughter asked.

"Yes, I did and I folded your clothes."

We made it to my room and I sat down on my bed and patted the spot next to me for Journee to have a seat.

"Journee Leigh I'm not going to go hard on you or yell at you because I want you to listen to me and take what I'm telling you to heart. I love you and you know that I'm only here for a little while. I raised you to be a phenomenal, independent woman.

I don't think that I could prepare you for life without me anymore than I already have. I'm so proud of you and I don't feel like I tell you that enough. You're a reflection of me but I must admit you're so wise, smart beautiful and you're more than I will ever be in life."

"Mother what's going on?" My daughter asked me, she started to cry.

"Don't cry Journee."

"Mother how can I not?" My daughter asked.

"Journee, let me say this because I'm not accusing you of anything. I'm just stating facts. I know you did something with Juelz today but I don't know what. You came home and you smelled like you took a fresh shower and cologne and you're tired.

That doesn't add up. Listen good Journee if Juelz isn't worth it, please don't give yourself to him. If he's worth it Journee, make him earn it. Make him work hard to get you."

"Mother, I haven't crossed that line with him yet. I promise you that. We have kissed that's it." My daughter explained.

"I hear you Journee. I'm not saying that Juelz isn't worth it because he could very well be your husband. What I will say is don't be blinded sided just because a nigga buys you nice and expensive shit don't be so quick to give in. You don't owe anybody shit. Anything a man can buy you, you can buy yourself. Pay attention and take heed to what I'm telling you. I love you and I'm here if you need any advice."

Journee didn't have sex with him but she did something she was like a deer caught in headlights. I didn't want to yell at her because I wanted her to tell me what's going on. I should face the facts that my baby is growing no matter what.

Journee

I had to hurry up and get out of my mother's room. I went to the kitchen to make my burger and drop me some fresh fries. It's like she was a psychic she could see right through me. Let's be honest if you told your mom that you just received oral sex from a nineteen-year-old would she still let him come through here Hell no. My mom played me now that I think about. I really like Juelz but I'm not ready to have sex with him yet.

I ate my food as fast as I could because I couldn't take another lecture without laughing and losing my cool. I forgot to text Juelz to let him know I made it home. I wish Nikki was home ain't no telling where she's at with Skeet. Ugh it sucks having only one friend. Oh well I don't deal with too many females anyway and Nikki didn't come with any drama we've been best friends since I was four years old.

"Journee where have you been?" My sister Khadijah asked breaking me out of my thoughts.

"I went out with a friend why? How was school today?"

"Journee is that guy your boyfriend? You don't tell me anything anymore. I don't like being left out the loop. I heard you and Nikki got to fighting up on the corner by the store. It's on YouTube somebody recorded y'all." My sister Khadijah asked.

"No, he's not my boyfriend yet. I'm not leaving you out the loop. Khadijah, you know you are my girl like a fresh bag of pearls. I would never leave you out. Give me a hug. I love you KD with your grown ass." I whispered in her ear.

"Journee I'm telling mother you cussed. I love you too. When are you taking me for a ride in that Benz?" My sister Khadijah stated.

"I'm taking you real soon."

I love Khadijah I swear that's my heart but she's too nosey trying to pick me for information. I cleaned and washed my plate. I headed to my room to find something to wear

tomorrow.

Chapter 12-Giselle

I'm so fucking livid right now. I've been laying around chilling all day. I didn't want to do shit today. Juelz hasn't been home in three days. I'm so stressed out. I don't know what the fuck to do. Ashley couldn't wait to rub it in my face that the little girl Journee was pushing a Benz truck with custom plates Juelz.

I wanted to smack her ass. She's the type of person that loves for you to be miserable because she is. She's a negative Nancy that's why I keep my distance and only tell her shit that I want her to know. I didn't believe her so the bitch sent me a picture as proof. I called his phone numerous of times to see what's up.

I didn't understand what Juelz would want with somebody in high school when he has a grown woman right in front of him. I need to know what's up because. I refuse to be out here looking dumb. Do you know how many guys are out here checking for me? I refused to give a bitch my meal ticket. I'm playing for keeps with him.

My auntie Mary called me and told me to come to Grady quick. Ashley is in the hospital she had a fight with Nikki and some girls on the corner of Hollywood and Simpson. She's in intensive care right now and it's not looking good. She was left for dead she got beat so bad her skull is fractured and she has blood on the brain.

Tears poured down my face I couldn't believe she done my cousin that dirty behind some dick. Ashley asked for it she kept fucking with that girl knowing damn well Skeet didn't want her. I got dressed quick to go see Ashley and comfort my aunt Mary.

I'm sure my whole family was as the hospital. I asked my aunt Mary where was her friends at and she stated two of them are in the hospital also. Nikki's friend beat them up. The only friend that Nikki had was Journee I heard. Ugh I'm starting not like this little bitch each day that passes.

It makes since now Nikki is probably the one who hooked Juelz up with Journee. Oh, she got me fucked up that's why she had an attitude and was laughing at me. She knew her friend was fucking with my man.

<u>Khadijah</u>

Ugh I'm so pissed off. Lately my mom has been letting Journee do whatever she wants to do. The guy Juelz who I assume is Journee's boyfriend has been hanging around our house more than usual. My mom keeps trying to tell me that they are just friends I'm not buying it. Ever since she started dealing with him she pops up with a new Benz truck nice jewelry you name it.

Today he brought his brother with him Smoke he's cool he's goes to my school he's in the eighth grade. I decided to be nosy and go outside and sit on the porch to see what was going on. My mom was in her room and Khadir went to the park with his friend.

Journee and Juelz were chilling and Nikki and Skeet was chilling and Smoke was sitting on the porch playing in his phone. I opened the door and he looked up. I sat in the chair with an attitude.

"What's up Khadijah." He stated in his deep voice.

"What's up Smoke it's KD to you not Khadijah."

"Yeah whatever Khadijah what are you doing over here." He asked.

"I live here this is my house?"

"Oh, you're Journee lil sister. I didn't know that."
He asked.

"It's a lot that you don't know about me."

"I know you need to stop hanging with Nisha and
Kay." He stated.

"Whatever Smoke, I just wanted to see why you
were on my porch. I'm going back in the house I'll see you
later."

"Juelz is my brother." He stated.

"Oh, ok good-bye Smoke."

"Khadijah don't leave sit out here and talk to me
until we leave." He asked.

"Boy, if my mother came out here and saw me
talking to you she would flip her wig if she had one. I can't
talk to boys Smoke." I laughed.

"Oh, your mother got you on lock? Shit when you're
at school you be acting fast when you are hanging with
Nisha and Kay. I couldn't tell that you were on lock but I
did notice you never come to the parties." He stated.

"You notice a lot huh." I pouted and folded my arms.

"Yep give me your number. I've been wanting it for a while but I thought you were fast like Nisha and Kay so I passed but I see you different just trying to fit in." He explained.

"Khadijah, what the fuck is you doing with a boy on my porch? Did I fucking miss something?" My mother yelled.

"Excuse me Mrs. Owens I'm Juelz brother Myshir. I'm in the eighth grade I do go to school with Khadijah but I didn't know that she was Journee sister." He explained.

"Juelz get yo knuckle head ass up here." My mother yelled.

"Yes Ms. Julissa." His brother Juelz asked.

"Look I'm going to tell your brother like I told you. Khadijah ain't nothing but thirteen ain't boyfriend and girlfriend shit up through here. You ain't slick now just because your brother was respectful I may consider letting him be Khadijah's friend, that's it nothing more nothing less. Do you understand me?" My mother voiced her opinion.

"Ms. Julissa, I know better I would never try to run game on you. I didn't know that the two of them even knew each other. My auntie is out of town this week so I'm babysitting." His brother Juelz stated.

"I'm watching y'all two. Juelz don't try me, you and Skeet. I'm on too y'all try me and see what happens." My mother stated and pointed her finger at the two of them.

"Your mother is mad crazy yo." He laughed.

"Tell me something I don't know, but I'll talk to you later Myshir."

"Khadijah where are you going? Give me your number so I can text you. Your mother said I could be your friend." He asked.

"I heard what she said but what makes you think that I want to be your friend because I'm not looking for any friends."

"Khadijah stop playing with me before I tell your mother what you really be doing at school with your fast as friends. I bet your mother don't know what Kay and Nisha be up too? I'll be glad to tell her that they're young hoes in the making and KD love to hang with them." He argued and gritted his teeth.

"Smoke you wouldn't."

"Oh, Khadijah I would I don't have nothing but time." He laughed.

"You're such a jerk. I can't stand you. I wish I would've kept my butt in the house."

"It's too bad go get your new friend some snacks and juice before I give your mother an earful and let me see your phone so I can get your math and text you my number." He laughed.

"Ugh I can't stand you I wish we had some bottle juice I throw it on you. You are working my last nerves. I'll be back."

I went in the kitchen to grab a juice and chips for Smoke. He bullied me out of my phone number.

"Um, Khadijah I heard what the fuck Myshir was saying about Nisha and Kay stop hanging with those young hoes because I don't ever want a motherfucker to mistake you as a hoe. Do you understand me? I don't like grown little girls and I refuse to let any of my children be a statistic." My mother explained.

"Yes, mother I understand."

"I'm glad you do, never be a follower Khadijah I bred leaders. Don't do what everybody else is doing that's exactly how I got pregnant with Journee trying to be grown and do what other girls my age was doing." My mother stated.

"I'm sorry mother." I batted my lashes and smiled.

"Yeah whatever Khadijah or should I call you KD go on back out there with your little friend and not boyfriend. Khadijah, I haven't whooped your ass in a long time. I'm feeling generous today keep being grown and watch what happens." My mother laughed.

I made my way back outside to see what Smoke was up too, he was all in my phone.

"Excuse you why are you going through my text messages like you are my boyfriend."

"Nice to see you too. Give me my snacks." He laughed and snatched the stuff out of my hands. I snatched my phone out of his hand.

"For somebody that can't talk to boys, you sure are talking to a few via text." He stated with his mouth full of chips.

"Why are you worried about it?"

"I'm not I sent those clowns a text and stated that you were talking to me and you couldn't talk to them anymore." He laughed.

"Why would you do that because you and me ain't talking?"

"I wanted too, you like those clowns or something your mother said you couldn't talk to boys but she said I could be your friend so we're talking." He laughed.

"Whatever Smoke, I don't want to talk to you and I really don't have too because my mother heard everything your big mouth said so you can cut it."

"Aye Smoke let's roll." His brother yelled.

"Bye Khadijah I'll call you later." He laughed and blew me kiss.

"No, you won't; I'm not answering" I laughed.

As soon as Juelz and Smoke pulled off he sent me a text.

Bae- You know you mine right

I couldn't do anything but laugh. He was too cocky for me. Smoke had a few hoes claiming him and I wasn't one to fall in line. Why would you text from my phone stating that I can't talk to whoever because of you?

"Khadijah, Smoke is cute let me find out that's your little boyfriend." My sister Journee stated.

"Journee he's not my boyfriend and you know that."

Smoke had sent me at least five text messages. We sent text after text to each other back and forth all day and night. I felt that this was the beginning of something.

Giselle

I didn't ask Juelz for much but dick, loyalty, and money that's it. Juelz and I were together but we weren't together. Y'all know how that shit goes. I asked him repeatedly was it anybody else and he said no. I knew better that nigga switched up like a thief in the night.

He stopped calling me and coming by. One day I came home just to check and see if he came by and the little things that he had here were gone. I called him to see what was up and he advised me that we needed space and we should date other people. I looked at the phone to make sure I wasn't tripping.

I asked him was he serious and he was like I'm so fucking serious. I politely hung up in his face. I couldn't believe him. It makes since now maybe Ashley was telling the truth about him and the Journee girl. If Juelz thought that he could leave me and be with Journee he's sadly mistaken. The paper that he chases every day is mine. That's one bag that I'm fucking securing. I'm not giving it up.

Before y'all even accuse me of being bitter that's not the fucking case. He lied to me I asked him was it somebody else and he said no. I cried to this man many of nights asking him what did I do wrong. He wiped my tears and beat this pussy up on numerous of occasions.

Since he's wants to lie to me about what's really going. I'm not going to be sorry about none of the shit that's about to transpire. Yes, I'm young I maybe a little dumb and childish but so what as far as I'm concerned Journee's a child. I'm going teach her a very valuable lesson about fucking with my man.

I'm going to teach Juelz a lesson also. He can never play me and think I'll accept everything that he's offering because I'm not. It's either me or her and trust me it's going to be me. I wouldn't have it any other way. I knew he was with Journee he never came out and said it.

I had to investigate on my own and I got my feelings hurt. I saw her and Juelz together he was happy and I hated it. You could only be happy for so long until I fuck it up. I wasn't having that; the streets were already talking. I would have the last laugh and it wouldn't be an Ashley situation.

***

A month later
<u>Chapter 13- Julissa</u>

To absent from the body and to be present with the Lord. Sunrise and Sunset. Everybody must die. When I first graced this world. I knew I wouldn't be here forever. I've been sick lately. I knew my time was coming. I just prayed that it wasn't today.

I've been in the hospital for two weeks. I've held on and fought for as long as I could but this ovarian cancer has taken a toll on me. I didn't have any more fight in me. I was tired and ready to go home. I wish my mother and I could've made amends but that's too much like right.

My children came to see my everyday it crushed my heart when they left today because I knew they wouldn't be back. This is the last time that we would see each other. I mustered up enough strength during the visit so I could love on them and tell them how much I love them.

Khadir, broke my heart, he said mommy when are you coming home? I miss you so much. I love you mommy and I hope you get better. Oh my God that shit broke my heart because it's not that simple. I've been in the hospital for two weeks and I knew the chances of me going home were slim to none. He laid in the bed with me and hugged me and cried. I held him so tight and rocked him to sleep.

A tear escaped Khadijah eyes I knew she was going through it too. She was being strong, I'm all they had and they're all I had. I hate to see my babies cry. I held Khadijah and kissed all over her pretty face. I told her that I loved her and to make the right decisions and listen to Journee I know this transition isn't going to be easy.

Journee Leigh, looked at me and smiled. I could see the gloss in her eyes and the tears threatened to run down her face she sucked it in. I knew my oldest child was hurting she was keeping together for the sake of her brother and sister. I prepared her for this day for months. I taught Journee everything that she needs to know about life.

I had no doubt in my mind that she wouldn't be good. It was almost 7:00pm and visiting hours were almost over. I kissed and hugged my kids. This was our final goodbye.

Journee

I prayed that this day would never come. My mom has been sick these past few weeks and in intensive care. Her battle with cancer has taken a toll on her body. Juelz has been at my side every step of the way.

I really didn't want to be around anybody. I just wanted to be by myself. Khadijah, Khadir and I just left the hospital. As soon as I got home and parked in the driveway. My phone rang it was the hospital.

"Hello."

"Hi Journee, this is Lisa your mother's nurse she just passed away as soon as you guys left her heart failed, we tried to revive her four times but she wasn't responding. I'm sorry for your loss. I'll gather her things for you and you can pick them up from the funeral home." My mother's nurse stated.

I hated to be on the receiving end of this call but we all must go someday. I'm glad my mother didn't suffer.

My heart crushed in a million pieces. I guess she waited until we left to die. I broke down in the car crying how am I supposed to explain this.

"Journee what's wrong?" My brother and sister asked.

"Let's go in the house give me a minute." I cried.

We made it into the house and I sat across the couch from Khadir and Khadijah.

"Mother is gone you guys she just passed away, as soon as we left."

My brother and sister cried like babies. My heart hurts for them. I don't have any parents my mother and father are both deceased. It's just me out here left to fend for myself. Lord knows they daddy ain't hitting on shit he left my mother for another woman and he doesn't handle any of his responsibilities.

I knew Khadir would take it the hardest because he's the youngest. Khadijah was crying hysterically. I hugged them both so tight and kissed the brim of their forehead. I wiped their tear ducts with both of my thumbs.

"It's going to be ok. I got y'all with everything in me. It's going to get better I promise you." I believe everything that I just told them. My mother always told me it greater later. I'm sure it would. I'm glad that all three of us got the chance to see her before she passed away. She knew what she was doing she was tired.

She fought as long as she could. My mother prepared me for this day for months now. I knew it was coming but I didn't want to accept it. My mother taught me everything she knew and some. I knew how to pay all the bills. The mortgage was on auto draft. She taught me how to be a young woman early.

I would miss her dearly and take every life lesson and skill with me to heart. These past few months we had so much fun I enjoyed every day that we spent together. Man, I'm going to miss my queen she was everything to me. The moment she laid eyes on Juelz she was on me like white on rice she was bloodhound, she knew everything.

I couldn't hide anything from her. My mother didn't want anybody to view her body she wanted to be cremated, she wanted to be with us every day. I respected that I would have her a small memorial at our church so people could pay her their respects.

I finally got Khadijah and Khadir situated. I ordered us some food. It was a little after 10:00 pm. I haven't spoken to Juelz all day normally we talk when he finishes handling business. I miss him. I should've called him earlier my mom really liked him.

I had to make to calls and notify her mother and let her know that she passed and make funeral arrangements. I couldn't believe her mother she had the nerve to say y'all can't stay here. Y'all must go to a foster home.

I had to correct her. I didn't call you to ask could I stay at your home. Julissa handled her business she made sure her three was straight and I was emancipated so it ain't no foster home for us. She pissed me off.

Ugh my mother was cut different so I could brag different. Let me call Juelz and see what he's up too.

"Hey baby, are you cheating on your man today." He laughed.

"Of course not. My mother passed away today."

"Journee are you, all right? You straight why didn't you call me earlier so I could be there for you. You know I got you. I have to make sure that you're straight. Khadijah and Khadir are they good?" He asked.

"I'm good I was going to call you. You know this is the time we normally talk anyway."

"Journee, I don't care about what we normally do. I must hold you down baby that's what I'm here for. I'm coming through so I can hold you. I love you." He explained.

"I love you too Juelz when are you coming?"

"I'm on my way give me about ten minutes. I need to stop by the Shell and get a few things and I'm pulling up." He stated.

**

Juelz made it exactly in ten minutes like he said he would. Khadir and Khadijah were asleep. He called me and told me to the open door.

"Hey you." He stated coolly.

"Hey, I'm in my room follow me."

"Lead the way." He smiled.

<u>Juelz</u>

I had to come and check on my baby. I can't believe she didn't call me as soon as she found out about her mother. I made it to her as soon as possible. I really liked Ms. Julissa she was the truth. You never knew what she was about to say. I would miss her. Journee wanted me to follow her to her room. I wrapped my arms around her waist so she could lead the way.

"Journee look at me are you good." I made her face me.

"I'm all right, I just can't believe it was this soon." She stated.

"I'm here for you. What do you need me to do? Give me a hug."

She cried on my shoulders. Journee loved her mother.

"Its ok baby I got you." I hugged her.

"I called my mother's mom to let her know that my mom passed away. Do you know she had the nerve to say? Y'all can't come here y'all must go to a foster home. It took everything in me to not curse this lady out. I only called her because my mom wanted me too." She cried.

"Stop crying baby as long as I'm breathing I got you and your brother and sister never question that." I wiped her tears with my thumbs.

"Thank you, but my mother made sure that we were straight when she left this world. She didn't want us to be a burden on anybody. She took care of her business and all of her responsibilities more than I can say for her own mother." She cried.

"Calm down baby it's cool I got you don't worry about it. Your mother wouldn't want you to be stressed and tripping about this."

"I am Juelz she didn't have any sympathy for her own child that's what pisses me off. I would never do that, show some respect." She cried.

"Everybody ain't real Journee and your mother was very real that's why she made sure you guys were straight. I'm about to get up out of here I'm tired. I'll see you tomorrow."

"No, you didn't hold me. I want you to stay with me or do you have something else to do?" She asked and pouted.

"Yo stop playing with me. You know I would rather be here with you than anywhere else."

"Good because I need to take a shower find us something to watch on TV I'll be right back." She stated. She grabbed her pajamas out of her drawer and headed to the bathroom.

"Hurry up I need to shower too. Don't run all the hot water out."

Chapter 14-Journee

Juelz was really a good boyfriend. I appreciate him more than he'll ever know. Whenever I call he's comes no questions asked. I loved that about him. The bathroom and the shower was my favorite place to relax and ease my mind. I heard a knock at the door. I knew it was Juelz. I don't want him to see me naked.

"Journee, you are using all the hot water let me get in with you really quick." He laughed.

"I don't think so."

"Journee, you don't have anything that I haven't seen before." He laughed.

"I have plenty that you haven't seen before."

"Are we really doing this right now come on. I'm getting in rather you like it or not." He explained.

I didn't even say anything because I didn't want to argue. I washed up quickly so I could get out soon as Juelz was making his way in.

"Stop you ain't going anywhere. I haven't seen you naked completely, but damn Journee I have eaten your pussy numerous of times and sucked your titties. I'm not going to do anything that you don't want me to do.

I haven't tried anything with you or forced you to do anything that you're not ready to do. I respect you. Even though I'm constantly getting blue balls" He yelled and gritted his teeth while grabbing the soap out of my hand.

"It's not that."

"Then what is it." He snarled.

"I'm sorry Juelz. I'm ready I been ready. I just didn't know how to say it. I just didn't want our first time to be here at the house and my brother and sister are in the next room. To make matters worse my mother just died. I always try to be respectful but I need you right now."

"Journee are you sure ready? If we take it there it ain't no turning back." He asked.

"I'm sure."

"I wanted our first time to be real special. I guess some things just happen that we can't prepare for." He stated.

"That's true."

I dried off and applied lotion my body with my Georgia Peach lotion from Bath Body Works. The scent was so strong it lingered in the air. Juelz stepped out of the shower and dried off also. I was exiting the bathroom and he called my name.

"Journee." He stated.

I turned around and looked at him.

"Yes."

"Wait up." He smiled.

I stood by the bathroom sink and waited for Juelz. He had the sexiest shade of caramel I ever saw on a man. I licked my lips the water was still glistening on his skin. His dick was swinging as he dried it off. He approached me and bit his lips. Juelz picked me up and carried me to my bedroom. He placed me gently on the bed.

"You know I've been wanting this for a long time. I promise to take it easy on you." He whispered in my ear as he sunk his teeth in my neck.

"I've been wanting it too." I ran my tongue across my lips.

"Don't let that tongue get you in trouble." He stated.

Juelz took his time with my body he traced his tongue down the middle of my breast and sucked each of them with so much passion. He traced his tongue further down my stomach and he bit the sides of my stomach. My legs were shaking and I started to squirm I was new to this.

"I got you Journee let me please you." He stated.

I shook my head ok.

He made his way down to my pussy I was familiar with the way his tongue felt down there. It was a euphoric feeling. He slid his tongue in and out of my opening at a very fast pace. I started to ride his face. He replaced his tongue with his dick.

"It hurts."

"Shh, I promise you I'm not going to hurt you." He whispered.

"Ok."

He slid the tip of his dick in out of me. It felt good all of sudden he slammed his dick inside of me. I screamed and he pressed his hand over my mouth.

"Journee you're going to have to take this dick it's yours and I want to give it to you. It's going to hurt at first but as you get used to it it's gone feel good. I'm gone take my hand off your mouth and do I what I do.

If you scream I really going to beat this pussy up. Do you want Khadijah and Khadir to hear you.?" He whispered in my ear.

I shook my head no. Juelz hit me with that smile that I love. Juelz started fucking me like he had something to prove. He threw my legs above my head and started nailing my pussy to the wall. The only sounds heard throughout the room where Juelz sliding in and out of me. My juices were flowing down the crack of my ass. I know my eyes had tear ducts in the crease of them. It didn't hurt as much but it didn't feel that good either.

"Turn around and arch your back." He stated.

I did as I was told Juelz grabbed me by hair and pulled me close to his chest and grabbed my ass and started hitting it front the back. It felt good but it hurts also. I started running from the dick. He placed both of his hands on my stomach to keep me in place his sweat dripped down my back. He dug his nails in my ass cheeks, he started pounding me from behind the only sounds heard echoing through the room where our bodies smacking each other and me trying to catch my breath.

"Juelz, slow down." I moaned.

"I'm trying to but this pussy too good. If I go to slow. I'll fuck around and nut. I'm not trying to do that." He stated.

Juelz

I've been wanting to break Journee off for a while now. I wanted more from her for than the pussy that hasn't been touched between her legs. I was willing to wait until she was ready. I couldn't believe that she was ready today of all days. Her pussy was so tight and wet it snatched a nigga soul. I thought I was about to bust as soon as I was in there. I'm selfish as nigga but I'm responsible. I wasn't strapping up.

I deserved this pussy. I wanted to feel all of it. I tried to take easy it on her but she was running from the dick. I didn't want to fuck her. I wanted to make love to her. I had to grab her stomach so she would be still and stop running. I grabbed her breast for support. I also wanted my way with Journee. I flipped her on her back we started tongue wrestling with each other.

The faces she was making and the way her juices coated my dick. I didn't have a choice but to beat this pussy out the frame.

"Get up there, I want you to ride me."

"It's too big Juelz." She pouted.

"You can handle it."

She got up there and I coached her on what to do. My hands gripped her ass. I palmed her ass in a circular motion forcing her to follow the rhythm I slid in and out of her. Her hands mounted my chest. She would be a natural after a few more sex sessions. She got the hang of riding me she started going at a fast pace.

I begged her to slow down. I didn't want to nut before her. I could feel her come all over my dick. I emptied my seeds in her. Rough sex is the best sex. I was tired I almost fell asleep in this pussy twice. Journee kept squirming each time she'll move she'll wake my dick back up.

"Did you nut Juelz and where?" She asked.

"I did I pulled out."

"Are you sure?"

We went round for round until I didn't have anything left in me. I got a warm towel and cleaned me and Journee up. She insisted that she take another shower. I'm glad she did because I forgot to pull out. It was too good I couldn't. I figured she knew I was lying. I'm a man and I'll take care of all my responsibilities.

Chapter 15-
Journee

Today was the day the we were honoring my mother with a nice Home-Going celebration. My mother stated before she died that she didn't want a funeral. Remember her how she was. Her friends reached out to me and insisted that we needed a celebration despite her wishes they wanted to celebrate her life one last time.

Who could forget Julissa Armstrong the one and only. The queen of all queens. My mother was perfect in every aspect she was mine and I'm her first creation. Tears cascaded down my face as I thought about her. She's everything to me and that'll never change. We wore white that was my mom's favorite color. My mother was loved in this community everybody loved her. Chapel Hill Baptist church was packed to capacity.

The whole hood came out to show love for my mother. She was loved my many and hated by plenty. Juelz came to the funeral with me he looked good in his all white True Religion. Khadijah looked nice too. She was starting to fill out. I would have to keep a close eye on her. I flat ironed her hair bone straight. I re-twisted Khadir dreads.

He was so handsome he was for sure to break some hearts. The service was scheduled to start 10:00am. My Godmother Valerie, Nikki and Skeet sat right behind us. My Godmother Valerie was grilling the shit out of me with that look like just because your mother is gone don't mean anything. She was my Godmother and she takes her duties seriously. She's been here every step of the way. I smiled at her. It was almost 10:00am the preacher had made his was way to the pulpit.

"Good Morning, we are here to celebrate the life of Julissa Armstrong she was beautiful soul. Can I get a round of applause and a standing ovation for her? Before I begin we are going to have a selection from the choir. Sister Troy will lead the solo Take me to the king." The preacher stated.

Take me to the king

I don't have much to bring

My heart is torn in pieces

It's my offering

Lay me at the throne.

"Sang it Troy go head now." My Godmother
Valerie yelled as she stood and held her hands up high and
swayed side to side.

I felt my mother's presence it felt so good.

"Give it up for sister Troy and the choir for the nice
selection. Julissa Armstrong, she was the queen of all
queens. Our community loved her. She had a very beautiful
spirit. To know her is to love her.

She didn't let what she was going through break her
or dictate her future. She fought until she couldn't fight
anymore. I saw Julissa a few days ago. The angels covered
her like the queen she was. She didn't want to talk but she
gave me a conversation despite the circumstances and she
dropped some knowledge.

I was thankful that I could see her one last time. The
good Lord has finally called my sister home. She was an
active member in church until she became ill but she still
came to church faithfully. We lost a beautiful soul but

Heaven gained an Angel our Angel. It's so much love in this room. I love, love. Deaths are blessing we lose one angel and another one is reborn again. Would anyone like to share any reflections are memories of Julissa." The preacher asked.

A few of my mother's friends went up and stated their fondest memories of my mother.

"I remember the first time I met Julissa in Bankhead Courts. I would never forget this day as long as I live. She was so pretty everybody said that she was stuck up because of Julian. I was getting jumped by three girls and my friends didn't jump in the just sat and watched.

Julissa didn't know me from a can of paint. I'm here to tell you Julissa got the chicks up off me and we started giving those girls the business we have been best friends ever since. I'm going to miss her." My Godmother Valerie stated.

"That's all y'all two did was keep some mess going." Somebody in the church yelled and laughed

Someone had tapped me on my shoulder I turned around and looked it was my grandmother and aunts waving. I gave them a faint smile.

Excuse my language I couldn't believe these bitches had the nerve to come to my mother's home going. To make matters worse they thought they had the privilege to sit up front with the family.

I haven't saw my grandmother and aunts maybe three or four times in my whole life. I just shook my head. Juelz could sense that something was wrong.

"What's wrong baby?" He whispered in my ear.

"My mother's mother and sister's just walked in." I whispered. Juelz put his arms around me.

"I would like to say something." My grandmother stated.

"Come forward." The preacher stated.

"I'm Julissa's mother many of you may not know. It wasn't the cancer that killed Julissa it's was the hard drugs that she did. I told her to leave that stuff alone. Now her kids are homeless and have to go to the state." My grandmother stated and the whole church shook their head in shock.

"Wait a minute. What you won't do is walk up in my mother's funeral and throw salt on her name. My mother ain't never done a drug a day in her life she refused chemo. From what I was told you have never been a mother to her or a grandmother to me.

For the record, my mother made sure her kids were straight while she was here and even when she's gone we're going to be straight. We'll never be homeless my mother took care of her business when it came to her children. Can you say the same? Don't ever speak foul on my mother's name." My sister Khadijah approached my grandmother and gave her the business.

She ran up out of here with her daughters behind her. Khadijah was my mother in every sense. They had no clue. I wasn't going to stop Khadijah she was respectful but nobody will talk about my mother foul and live to tell about it.

The preacher said his final remarks the Home-Going Celebration was nice despite my grandmother coming to show her ass but in return Khadijah gave it to her like my mother would. I noticed Khadijah's and Khadir's father on our way walking out.

"I'm sorry for y'all lost. Can I speak with y'all for minute?" Their father stopped us and stated.

"We don't want to talk." My brother and sister stated.

"Khadijah and Khadir its ok hear the man out y'all good. I got y'all we got each other."

"I'm sorry about how things went down. I'm here for you two and if you need anything let me know." Their father stated

"We need some money for school clothes and shoes." My sister Khadijah explained.

"Ok that's cool I'll give both of you guys $500.00 a piece is that enough?" Their father asked and pulled out a wad full of cash.

"Make it $700.00 a piece since you haven't been around in a while." My sister Khadijah stated.

"Ok that's fine, take my number down and call me. I want to be a part of y'all lives. I could never leave you guys again. I'm sorry and I'll spend the rest of my life making it up to you. Journee, make sure you call me if you need help with them. I'll come get them. Let me give you $700.00 also." Their father stated.

"Ok that's fine Mr. Owens I'll be glad too."

"Journee call me KD ok I'm old but not that old." Their father laughed.

Khadijah

My mother had a nice Home-Going service. It was so much love in the church it didn't make sense. I couldn't believe my grandmother had the audacity to speak on my mother's name like that. I don't know if Journee was going to speak up but I was. Ain't a woman alive that can take my mother's place.

My mother didn't even do her chemo treatments and that possibly could've saved her life but you had the nerve to insult her. Oh no I wanted to cuss her ass out and use curse words but I thought I'll be a little respectful even though she disrespected us. I was glad my dad came to support us I really appreciated that.

I'm sure my mother would be proud. I broke his ass in case I didn't see him again. I had a feeling this wouldn't be our last time seeing him. Khadir was so mean he's normally the nice one. He doesn't know him so of course he has his guard.

I was tripping off My Godmother Valerie. My mother ain't ever told us that story. It's seems like history was repeating itself that's Nikki and Journee. I am going to miss my queen so much. My hearts hurts badly the day she left me. She's my guardian Angel and I know Journee is going to take care of us. Nothing will change but I'm going to miss laying in my mother's bed and laying up under her. Her room smells just like her.

"Khadijah and Khadir it was good seeing your father today." My sister Journee stated.

"It was I was glad to see him. I can't lie."

"Forget him. Why did we wait until my mother died to show his face?" My brother Khadir asked.

"I don't know Khadir but life is too short. I don't have any parents my mother and father are both gone at least you guys have somebody. If he wants to have relationship with you guys let him." My sister Journee stated.

"I hear you Journee."

"I hear you too." My brother Khadir stated.

The rest of the ride home we continued to talk and reminisce about our mom it was just the three of us no matter what. Yes, my father was alive but we were all that we had. Our mother had family but y'all see how her family gets down.

Chapter 16-Giselle

You can call me Carmen San Diego I'll be all of that. I've been watching Journee for the past month. I've been waiting on the perfect time to approach her regarding Juelz and me. I had to crush her heart because the nigga broke mine and took me for granted. Mr. Perfect ain't so fucking perfect. I'm a calculated bitch I always make my next move my best move.

I knew everything about little Ms. Journee and I mean every fucking thing. Bankhead is a small and bitches will talk for a drink and some loud. Money wasn't an issue because I still had bands on demand courtesy of Juelz. Despite what he tells everybody and makes it seems to the public. It's still me and him. He spends at least three nights a week at my house. I snapped a few pictures up for proof. It was Ben Hill day and everybody was out.

My cousin Keionna and Meka were posted up on the block and sent me pictures of Juelz and Journee riding on his dirt bike. I was swinging by there. I was already coming down Campbellton Rd. It would take me about fifteen minutes to get where Ben Hill Day was located. Anytime I stepped out of the house I was dressed to impressed and today was no different. My makeup was freshly done. I got my hair sewed-in on Saturday. My hair was bone straight. I got my nails and Pedi done this morning.

I had a fitted Chanel Canary yellow maxi dress on that stopped right above my thigh. I opted for a pair of nude Chanel sandals. I had my big Chanel frames on. The two of them disgust me. I wanted to throw up. I spotted Nikki and Journee and Skeet and Juelz. He was booed up with the bitch I could tell he was in love with her by the way he looked at her.

The sight of them added fuel to the fire that hasn't been put out. I played the background I couldn't show out here because I knew Juelz would put his hands on me. He didn't have a hand problem but he would choke me out if he knew I was in the business of jeopardizing his relationship. I was letting shit be known today.

I couldn't stand the site of them two. Journee Leigh would see me. I would be at her doorstep tonight. I made my way out of their I bumped the fuck out of Journee on my way out. She tried to push me and I sped up and ran toward my car. It was funny my ass was jiggling. I had a date anyway.

***

Journee finally made it home. I watched her pull in her garage with two kids who I assume was her brother and sister. Her truck was nice as fuck. Unlike my Lexus that had many dents that Juelz refuses to get fixed, but her car was in good condition.

I was parked down the street. I let her get in a few minutes before I knocked on her door and ruined her life with my man. I had the same clothes on from earlier. I hope she recognized this Canary yellow dress.

I pulled up in front of her house like I owned the motherfucker. I banged on her door like I was the fucking police. I heard someone come to the door. A little girl that looked like Journee snatched the door.

"Bitch why are you banging on our fucking door like you're the police, what the fuck you want?" Her sister yelled with an attitude.

"Is Journee here?"

"She is but what the fuck do you want with Journee you ain't Nikki my cousin. I ain't never seen you around here what you want?" Her little sister argued.

"I'm a friend, we went to school together I was in the neighborhood."

"Yeah right. Journee some bitch I ain't never seen before at the door asking for you." Her sister yelled in my face.

I heard Journee yell in the background and ask her sister who was at the door. This little girl here was too damn grown she need her ass beat.

"Khadijah stop all of that cussing like you grown. What's up do I know you? You're the same bitch from earlier that pushed me at Ben Hill Day what's up." She sassed.

"This conversation could go one or two ways. We could talk like women or we could fight. It didn't matter to me I had Vaseline in my purse."

"First, you 're at my house on my doorstep talking shit. Shawty I don't know you. You can clear it." She stated.

"Oh, you don't know me but we have something in common Juelz." I had her attention now.

Journee

Giselle is a bold bitch. You have the nerve to come to my house and bang on my door like you are the police. To make matters worse you're the same chick that pushed me at Ben Hill Day. I never forget faces ever and here you are today on my doorstep with that same loud ass yellow dress.

I don't bother anybody but I don't like this chick's vibe at all. I don't like being disrespected or confronted. I will defend myself at all cost, if she gets besides herself. I will beat the black up off this chick. My mother just passed away and I don't need anybody thinking its ok to come to my home. She said we had one thing in common and that's Juelz.

"I'm guessing you're Juelz EX what do you want with me and why are you at my house? You saw me and Juelz at Ben Hill Day why didn't you approach me there?"

"I've never been Juelz EX I'm his main and you know that. I don't know what y'all two got going on but it stops today." She sassed.

"Hold up, Khadijah grab my phone."

"Ok." She stated.

"It's Giselle, right? You look silly coming to my house about my man. Why not approach him he's your issue not me? It's always good to check the man before you call yourself checking a female you know nothing about."

"Silly, listen little girl. I know everything about your hoe ass. You like fucking grown men for money and men that are already in a relationship. I know your kind well. Everybody knows that Juelz is mine you're just the boldest bitch to ever think that you could fuck with him and I wouldn't get at you.

Let's make some shit clear you're the one that's fucking silly. I fuck Juelz every day. He's stays at my house at least three times a week. I thought you were smart and I wouldn't have to break it down to you but check out this video of me and my man." She sassed and smirked.

I couldn't believe this. Juelz was still fucking Giselle and this was recent because he had that shirt on yesterday. It's a wrap I'm not fucking with him anymore and to make matters worse she asked him on the video did he fuck with me and he denied it.

"I didn't mean to hurt your feelings but Juelz is my man." She laughed.

"You can never hurt my feelings. I'm never pressed by any man to show up at another female's house asking questions. If you must do all of that to prove a point. He ain't worth it. You still look stupid and dumb. What you can do is get your stupid self-up off my porch and see your way out."

"Stupid, nope baby girl that'll be you again. Your dead ass momma should've schooled you and told you to never fuck a grown man with some money and in a committed relationship." She laughed as she was up in my face picking with me.

This hoe thought that she had the upper hand. I pushed her with so much force. She fell on my porch. I walked over to her with my fist balled up. I punched her in her forehead with so much force. I heard her neck snap back. I wasn't finished yet. I grabbed her by her long as Remy hair and rammed her face into the brick pavement on my house.

"Journee Leigh beat her ass." My sister Khadijah yelled. Hyping me up.

I wasn't finished yet; this was just the beginning. I rammed her face so much into the brick structure you could see the white meat. She begged me stop.

"Can you please stop." She cried.

"Nope you shouldn't have brought your stupid ass over here."

I started stomping her out me and Khadijah. Khadijah kicked her in her mouth and head. I was so tired and out breath. I called Juelz he answered on the first ring.

"Hey baby, what's you good you want me to come through?" He asked.

"Juelz do you have anything that you want to tell me."

"No why." He asked.

"Juelz I'm not even about to beat around the bush with you. You are a fucking liar and I'm so done. Giselle came to my fucking house, to confront me about you and she showed me a video of you and her fucking and she asked you about us and you denied it.

She's still here. I beat the shit out of her. Get this bitch off my porch now, you have ten minutes and if you're not here I'm slicing this bitch up and feeding her to my fucking dogs." I hung up in his face I don't want to hear shit that he's has to say.

Khadijah

I don't know what's going on but Journee beat the shit out the girl that came to our house. I called Nikki so that she could come by to see what was going on. She said that she was with Skeet and she was on her way.

I'm nosey I don't care this chick was disrespectful and rude. I heard her say something about my mother being dead I lost it and Journee did too. I called Nikki back and she answered on the first ring.

"Yeah Khadijah." My cousin Nikki asked with an attitude.

"Where you at Journee beat the shit out of that Giselle girl she's on the porch leaking."

"Khadijah stop cussing you ain't grown. I'm on my way so the girl was Giselle?"

"Yes, she was rude and nasty she had the nerve to say something about my dead ass momma. It was on from there. She got served."

"Khadijah I'm pulling up now. Where's Journee?" My cousin Nikki asked.

"She's taking a shower."

"Ok let me in." My cousin Nikki told me.

Chapter 17-Juelz

I fucked up and I fucked up good. Giselle played me. I played myself. I couldn't stop fucking her. She had the nerve to record me and her fucking and show Journee the video. What type of shit is that?

I kept replaying Journee last words in my head. If I lose Journee behind Giselle childish ass she'll regret ever fucking with me. How do you even know where she lives? What made you go to her house?

***

I made it to Journee's house in exactly ten minutes. I was up on Hollywood Rd. It didn't take me that long to get around here. I didn't want Journee to kill Giselle it wasn't that serious. Skeet and Nikki was already here.

Skeet was sitting in his car. I guess Nikki was in the house. I jumped out of my car and ran to Journee's house and Giselle was laid out on the porch passed out. She still had a pulse. I cut the water hose on and sprayed Giselle ass so she could wake up and get the fuck on. Nikki was standing in the doorway and shook her head.

"Giselle let's go who told your dumb ass to come over here anyway starting drama. If you would've died, then what."

"Juelz, you played me." She argued.

"How and bitch I'm not your man. Journee is my girl. Take your dumb ass on. Don't call me no more."

"I'm not leaving here without you." She argued.

"Giselle take your ass home. If you think that you're about to stay at this girl's house you have another thing coming. I will have Journee to beat your ass again. Go home now."

I went to the truck to holler at Skeet.

"You got hoe problems." My right-hand man Skeet laughed.

"You ain't never lied. Giselle set me up." We slapped hands with each other.

"What happened?" My right-hand man Skeet asked.

"Man, I don't even really know. Journee called me and asked did I need to tell her anything. I said no then she went in about Giselle showing her a video of me and her fucking. They fought and she told me I have ten minutes to pick this bitch up before she slice and dice her. Giselle said she wasn't leaving unless I was. I damn near broke her neck." I ran my hands across my face. I fucked up.

"Get your shit together, go check on Journee and tell Nikki to come on." My right-hand man Skeet stated.

I walked to the door and opened it. I went to Journee room and Nikki stopped me at the door.

"Juelz, she doesn't want to speak to you. It's best that you leave. Tell Skeet I'm spending the night and I'll call him." Journee best friend Nikki stated.

"You tell Skeet yourself just like Journee can tell me herself."

Nikki walked out. I closed Journee's room door and locked it. She was laying down on her bed.

"Can we talk?"

"Talk Juelz but you only got three minutes." She yelled.

"I'm sorry and I fucked up."

"Is that all, if so, you can leave and don't come back lose my number." She argued and sassed.

"Journee, I promise you I didn't try to hurt you. I went over her house to get my stuff and I fell asleep and it just happened."

"Juelz, it is what it is. Your explanation isn't good enough for me. The fact remains the same you had sex with her. This is the same chick that shoved me at Ben Hill day that I was telling you about.

Not only that, she came to my house because of you and we fought. I'm not stepping out of character behind a man. It's not worth it. Do you know how much anger I have built up inside of me I could've killed her? I'm not jeopardizing my family for none of this. It was fun while it lasted but we are done here." She stated.

"But Journee listen to me really quick."

"Ain't no buts Juelz, I don't want to hear your excuses I'll see you when I see you." She put her hand up and stated.

"I'm sorry."

I apologized I don't know what else to do. I fucked up damn. I hurt Journee and I never wanted to do that. I never thought this shit with Giselle would bite me in the ass so fast that'll I miss a good thing before it could start.

Journee was so serious she couldn't even look at me. I promise you if Journee chooses not to be with me behind this shit. Giselle thought she got her ass beat. I will pay some hoes to beat her ass.

Nikki

I can't believe Juelz. Giselle is a bold lame as bitch like her cousin Ashley. To make matters worse you shoved Journee at Ben Hill day with that same loud as dress that you got your ass handed to you in. Journee don't even bother anybody she minds her business she's quiet but wake up the beast that's hidden and it's a wrap.

Khadijah recorded the fight. Giselle couldn't even fight with all that mouth. As soon as I ran on the porch and this dumb chick was still laid out on the porch I kicked her in her face. I wanted to pick up the chair and dump on her but I knew Skeet was watching me like hawk. Journee is better than me I would've killed that bitch for coming to my house.

I heard the bitch begging Juelz to leave with her and he wasn't, she said that she wasn't leaving either. I wanted to yell out the window and tell that hoe she better get the fuck on before I beat her ass my damn self.

Skeet was mad that I was spending the night with my best friend. She needed me more than him. My best friend comes before anything her mother just passed so I'm going to be here with her if she needs me to be. I can only imagine how she feels. We just laid in the bed and I rubbed her back.

"Journee I'm sorry for introducing to Juelz. I thought he was different."

"Nikki it's not your fault that he was still fucking her. You kept it real from jump about her. It's all good before school starts I'm moving to Duluth. I'm buying a home." My best friend Journee revealed.

"Why Journee don't move because of him?"

"It's not because of him but his actions did give me the extra push. Nikki, you have moved with your future husband you don't stay up the block anymore. I want Khadijah and Khadir to have a better education and I'm tired of the shit that's going on around here.

I've already been looking at houses. With my mother being gone I really don't want to stay here Nikki I'm about to paint this house and rent it out. I would never sell it. If I stay here I'll lose focus and Juelz will woo me back and I can't be wooed. It's somebody for everybody and he ain't for me." My best friend Journee revealed.

"I'm going to miss you Journee so much. Ugh I can't stand Juelz got my best friend moving over in Gwinnett

County. I don't agree with what are you doing because I feel like you're running away from him but I support you no matter what.

I don't want to be in the middle of your drama. Journee, you should still hear him out just for closure if you are really done with him." I gave her the side eye I don't think Juelz tried to hurt her he just slipped up. If he really cared about Giselle, he would've never put his hands on her.

"Nikki put yourself in my shoes how would you feel? Would you forgive Skeet so quick?" My best friend Journee asked.

"Hell, no I would kill his ass and his jump off and then bring him back to life to kill his again."

"I wouldn't do all of that. The only thing that I'm going to do is focus on Journee Leigh and move on. You live and you learn but I'm good I don't need to hear Juelz out. I've heard enough and seen too much so I'm good.

If Giselle is doing all of that. I damn sure don't want no parts of that because the next time it'll be murking season and not another ass whooping. It's cool I enjoyed beating the snout out of her. I'll pick of the pieces." My best friend Journee stated.

Nikki

Skeet and I finally moved in together. I loved me some Skeet that nigga so fine. He had all these bitches going wild, but I had him all of him. I had that nigga by the balls. He was perfect. Bright skin, body covered in tattoos, nice teeth. Jet black hair with deep waves adorned his head. Dark eyes, mustache goatee. He had thick build he was muscular. I loved when he picked me up. Most of all I loved that pipe that laid between legs and touched the middle of his thigh.

I finally got my BMW X5. I wasn't playing with him. We've been dating for nine months and I'm carrying his first child. Oh yeah, I made him give up that bachelor's pad too.

Ashley was still in ICU her mammy was pissed. She called herself running down on me and Skeet talking shit. Like mother like daughter. I popped that old bitch in her eye one good time. She was still talking shit I popped that bitch in her mouth, then I called my mother Valerie Dallas because I don't have time.

She pulled up and showed her ass like I knew she would. She don't play no games about me period. Skeet was mad but nobody is going to disrespect me period. I don't give a fuck how old they are. I was raised to respect my elders but respect goes both ways respect me and I'll respect you. Once Skeet learns that will be perfectly fine. If I get action trust me I'm reacting.

He brought us a big house in Douglasville with five bedrooms and three bathrooms. I didn't need a house that big. Who in the fuck was going to be cleaning up all of this shit? Not me. I didn't mind decorating the house because I'm going to school for Interior Design.

Skeet said that since I gave him his first child I had to give him four more. I was the only women that was going to have that title. I don't want no more. I need a ring before I pop out any more children. My mother was mad at first but she accepted it. She respected him for stepping up and doing what he has to do for us.

My father is about to get out of the FEDS in a few weeks Nick Williams. I didn't even want to tell my father that I was pregnant but my mom insisted. How do you tell your father that you're seventeen and pregnant? My dad is pretty cool but we'll see once he gets out but Skeet is a standup guy. I couldn't ask for a better father for my child.

Chapter 18-Juelz

I feel so defeated and helpless. I couldn't wait to get Giselle's condo. I hate to put my hands on a female but she asked for everything that's coming to her tonight. First, you recorded us fucking that's a no no. You got my business out in the streets. If I recorded, you sucking my dick from the back you'll be mad.

You went to this girl's house like you big and bad picking with her on some old childish shit, I can't fuck with you no more you need to grow up. You are running around acting like a hoe. When I make it to your house I'm going to fuck you and treat you like a hoe and record you and show some niggas since you call yourself putting me on blast and fucking up my relationship.

This is one of the main reasons why I don't want to be with you because you childish as fuck and you need to grow up instead of running up behind me. You need to get some business about yourself. Journee is seventeen and way more mature than her. She's not focused on what I'm doing and who she's focused on her brother and sister she has real responsibilities. I can't wait to see her desperate ass.

***

I made it to Giselle's condo in about thirty minutes. I banged on her door like I was the fucking police and I was kicking her door also. She swung the door open with a scowl on her face. I pushed passed her.

"Juelz why are you doing this to me." She pouted with an ice pack on her head.

"It doesn't feel good, does it?"

"Juelz, how do you think I feel? You can fuck me Monday through Sunday but you have a girlfriend and you still fucking on me. It's not me that's making things complicated it's you. Yes, you broke up with me to be with her.

You cheated on me with her. You broke my heart. You put your hands on me because I asked you about her. So yes, I had to get at her the best way I knew how to let HER know that I'm still in the picture and I'm not sorry. I hope she leaves your dog ass and never takes you back. I'm not backing down that easy and letting you be with her." She argued.

"Giselle, cut that bullshit out. I ain't pressed for no pussy because Journee is a virgin and her pussy fits me like a glove. I'm the first nigga to break it in and I'll be the last nigga to touch it. I'm not fucking you because I want too, bitch you are fucking begging me to fuck you.

I gave your key back and took all my shit to my spot. You call me over here every day for small shit and throw pussy my way. Giselle I'm not a dumb ass nigga I know you be fucking different niggas. I saw you at the park and I watched you jumped in the car with ole boy.

I had Lonzo follow your hoe ass and guess what he pulled on the side street and you were fucking a nigga in the same dress you got on but you wanted to fuck with my girl on some hoe shit and you out her fucking other niggas.

I'm going to treat you like a hoe and fuck right behind that nigga. Lonzo said you were fucking him real nasty too. He showed me the pictures how you were fucking ole boy. I had to take my glasses off. You can never play a nigga like me and think you got one up on me.

I don't fucking want you. You want to know why because you ain't shit but a sack chasing hoe. Get up off my sack hoe, bend that ass over so I can see what this pussy does one last time."

"Juelz I'm sorry let me explain. I was trying to." She cried and explained before I cut her off.

"Giselle, you don't have shit to explain to me. I can't trust you the only thing you can do right now is fuck me like you know it's going to be your last time. It's your last time. Go wash your pussy so I can think about how I'm supposed to get my girl back."

"Juelz did you just say what the fuck I thought you said? You got me so fucked up." She argued and sassed.

"Giselle if you can what you can hear. You heard right what's the issue you been fucking that nigga and me at the same time what's the difference now? The only difference now is that I caught you red handed. You can't do what I do.

Do you want the dick or not? If not let me know and I can leave and go beg Journee to take me back and suck on her pussy, all night or you can fuck me like a porn star and shut the fuck up. You've already been talking too much. So, what's it going to be?"

"Let me go take a shower I'll be right back." She pouted.

Giselle so dumb and stupid I shouldn't even fuck her because she's so fucking desperate and she doesn't have any morals. You know what fuck this shit I'm leaving fucking her ain't gone solve shit.

Let me take my ass home but before I go back home let me see if Journee will at least talk to me. I know she has had some time to cool off. I slammed the door and hopped in car and peeled off and made my way back to Journee's.

Giselle

I took a hot shower and cried in the shower like I was baby. Juelz talked to me like I was hoe and just straight trash. I had no clue that he knew I was fucking with Free, I'm crying because I got caught. Free and I just happened, this nigga here has some major paper he's from the West Side too but he hangs out by Summerhill.

I didn't think Juelz and Skeet knew him. I met him at the Mexican off Old National Pkwy with Ashley a few months ago. When I tell you that niggas bread is long and he doesn't mind bussing down. We've fucked more than a few times but he has a situation like I do. He has a girl and I did have man. I like everything about Free and I love what that nigga can do for me. Free is everything that Juelz isn't he's makes time for me and I feel like we're dating.

His girlfriend is in the army and she's stationed overseas so majority of the time when Juelz is out doing him I'm with Free. He's taking me to Miami this weekend. Juelz is really feeling that little young bitch she had a lot of heart. I couldn't believe he told me he would eat her pussy all night and beg her to take him back. He has never given me head in the year that we've been fucking around. I cut the shower off to go find Juelz.

"Juelz."

I didn't hear him I dried off and lathered my body with some Sweet Pea lotion. I wrapped a towel around my body and headed downstairs to find Juelz and guess what this bastard was gone. He didn't give a fuck about me.

I got my ass beat and he couldn't even console me. I should take a warrant out on Journee but I couldn't because I came to her house. I don't even feel as bad now that Lonzo watched me fuck Free and showed Juelz. I can't believe him let me call Free and see if he can't get us a room.

Juelz

We supposed to be in love, til it ain't no breaking up.

I've been calling Journee she hasn't been answering any of my calls. I know that she needed time to cool off but fuck that she has had enough time. I called Skeet to see where Nikki was he said that she was down there. He had an attitude, if it's that's serious go get her. I told him to meet me down there.

***

I made it over Journee's in about thirty minutes. Skeet was already outside and Nikki was sitting in the truck that was my que to go in and Skeet to pull off and took Nikki home because I needed to speak with Journee alone.

I know how Nikki is I don't need her judging me and she don't know our situation. I walked in Journee house and locked the door. I made my way to her room, she had her back turned and she was crying. I took my clothes off quietly and climbed inside of the bed with her. I wiped her tears and whispered in her ear.

"I'm sorry what a nigga gotta to do make shit right Journee."

She ignored me and continued to cry.

"I'm sorry man stop crying please I didn't mean to hurt you." I turned Journee around on her back so she could face me. I wanted her to see how sorry I was. I was hurting because she's hurting.

"Journee look at me I'm sorry and I promise I'll never hurt you again. I'm hurting too because you're hurting. I vowed to be your first and last everything. All I'm asking is forgiveness and another chance to prove to you that I'm that nigga. I fucked and I'm man to enough to admit that. I'm man enough to say I'm sorry and it won't happen again. I refuse to let a good thing pass me bye."

"Juelz if I cheated on you with another man and he recorded us having sex and showed you, tell me how you would react it? Would you forgive me?" She argued.

"Journee, you got me fucked, hell no I would kill your ass and then forgive you at your funeral." I yelled and gritted my teeth.

"That's how I feel Juelz. I forgive you but I would never forget and for that reason alone that's why I'm choosing to move on. I don't want to have nothing to do with you. It was too easy for you to cheat and we've only been together a little over six months.

We could've stayed friends but nope you crossed that line and broke my heart in the process. I love you Juelz and sometimes the hardest things in life to do are for the best." She explained and turned her back against me.

"I love you Journee no matter what you'll forever be mine and don't even think about bringing another nigga in the equation. It'll be some slow singing and flower bringing."

I tried to turn her around so she could face me

Journee mind fucked me and played me at my own game with this reverse psychology shit. She broke up with me. I'll give her space but she couldn't have another boyfriend. I ate Journee's pussy like my life depended on it.

I sucked the soul out of her. I was determined to get her back just the thought of another man trying to be with her fucked me up and I couldn't take. Yes, I had some shit to prove.

"Let me put the tip in."

"Juelz do you actually think that I would sleep with you and you've been cheating on me with her? I may be young but never will I be dumb behind any man. Can you leave please you are making things more complicated? Grab the keys to the Benz you can get that jewelry too." She pouted.

"Anything that I ever brought you it was from the heart and I wanted you to have it. I would never take anything back from you. I love you Journee and I'm not going to stop trying to get at you." I put my clothes and left Journee and I locked eyes with each other. For some reason, it felt like this would be my last time seeing her the way she looked at me.

Chapter 19-Journee

I couldn't wait to curse Nikki out she set me up as soon as Skeet called she went outside and never came back and Juelz came in and got in the bed with me. Juelz was sorry I forgive but I will never forget. I'm not a basic female and I refused to be. We are all human and we all make mistakes. You didn't care about continuing to sleep with Giselle you wanted your cake and ice cream too.

If I would've took him back and had sex with him. He would continue to fuck her and me too but it's not that type of party. He would thank me later. I appreciated the head it was amazing but I must move on.

He didn't appreciate what we had so going forward I would learn to live my life without him. You know what they say you'll never miss a good thing until it's gone. Trust me he'll miss me when I'm gone and I'll miss him too but eventually I get over it.

***

To say I was hurt was an understatement. I love Juelz, was I in love with him probably so. I can't even lie. Who am I kidding I was in love with him and he broke my heart. My heart hurts so badly. Lord please take the pain away. It aches and only Juelz can take this pain away.

I only cry when I'm in the shower because I don't want Khadijah and Khadir to hear me. I wish my mother was here for this. I should've kept my guard up; he broke all my barriers down. To love and to lose. Juelz has been calling me non-stop leaving me voicemails and text messages begging to have a conversation. I just watch the phone ring. I refuse to answer I don't have anything to say.

I miss him but I can't give in I refuse too. It's hurt too much and I don't like to look like a fool. Hopefully, everything will be better once I move. I can't wait to start over and get my fresh start.

I'm still trying figure out what I'm going to do with this truck because I don't want it anymore and he refuses to take it back. I'm getting a PO BOX all my mail will be forwarded. I don't want to deal with anything associated with Juelz.

***

The move to Gwinnett was peaceful. I liked living out here. It wasn't much movement. School was scheduled to start on August 9th. I was going to home-school for my senior year because even though I'm emancipated High School starts earlier than expected and I need to be here in the morning to take Khadijah and Khadir to school.

I could do my classes online. I had more than enough credits to graduate I would be walking across the stage in December. I hate that my mother wasn't here to witness that but I'm sure she'll be proud. I would miss Nikki dearly but I'm sure we would talk everyday that'll never change. I can't wait until my Godson makes his appearance in the world.

I found a very nice family to rent my mother's house out to. I made sure to let the tenants know if anybody comes by here particular Juelz to not give any information. My mother and I had a joint account at SunTrust the tenants would deposit the rent money in there every month. I purchased us a nice home very good subdivision.

I changed my number because Juelz couldn't get the picture that it was over. I got Khadijah a new phone also I didn't want her keeping in contact with Smoke. She didn't understand what was going on but I had to tell her we needed to focus and make our mother proud because Smoke and Juelz was a distraction.

I missed my hood Bankhead because it was always something going on I'm adapting to change. I love Juelz he will always have a special place in my heart but I love him enough to let him go so he can do him and I can do me. It's so hard but I refuse to give in and be that female that a guy cheats on and she takes him back.

Juelz

I decided to give Journee some space. I knew me cheating on her was hard and a lot to deal with because I was her first everything. I noticed a for rent sign in front of her mother's home two weeks ago. I didn't pay it any mind.

I decided that two weeks was too long to be away from each other. I knocked on the door I had two dozen roses and some diamond earrings. I heard some footsteps and an older lady came to the door.

"Hi sir, how may I help you?" The older woman asked.

"I'm looking for Journee can you get her?"

"Sir Journee moved and I'm renting out this house from her." The older woman stated.

"Do you have her number?"

"I do but she told me not to give it out and important people that need to contact her have it. I'm guessing you're the man that broke her heart?" The older woman asked.

"I'm not that guy. I appreciate the information."

I walked back to my car and looked back at the house one last time. I can't believe Journee up and left me and didn't say shit. I felt my chest tighten I guess she was feeling like I was. I had to call Skeet because I know Nikki knows where she moved too. How did I miss that she moved? Who helped her move and why didn't Skeet tell me shit? I need some answers because I had a shit load of questions. I called Skeet right up.

"Yo Juelz what's good?" My right-hand man Skeet stated.

"Damn why you didn't tell me that Journee moved and rented out her mom house?"

"I didn't know Nikki didn't tell me shit." My right-hand man Skeet explained.

"Put Nikki on the phone."

"Yes Juelz. "She stated.

"Damn Journee moved and you couldn't tell me anything?"

"Juelz, I tried to stop her from moving but she refused to listen to me. She said that she was thinking about moving anyway and I guess the breakup and you cheating gave her the push that she needed." She sassed.

"What's her phone number?"

"She didn't give it to me because she knew that I would give it to you. Juelz, Journee is so hurt behind that shit. She was sick and throwing up. Giselle was playing on her phone playing the boy is mine and sending that video to her phone doing all types of childish shit." She stated.

"Where did she move too?"

"She brought a house in Gwinnett. "She stated.

"Why did she move way out there?"

"She said the schools were good and she wanted a better opportunity for Khadijah and Khadir." She explained.

"Who sold her the house?"

"Juelz, I don't know all of that. I think it's something that she wanted to do for a long time because before she found out about you and Giselle she was already looking at houses and had that one picked out." She explained.

"All right Nikki good looking out. If she calls you tell her I love her and I'll find her. Tell Skeet I'll hit him back later."

Damn it's going to be hard to find Journee in Gwinnett County they operate a little different than Fulton county. Our tax assessors in Fulton County are mostly black versus being in Gwinnett County majority white.

Giselle is still on that bullshit, why and you fucking and sucking another nigga? It's cool for you to do you but if I'm doing me it's a problem you're still fucking with that girl after she beat the snot out of you.

I don't even hit women but I should smack the fuck out of Giselle just off the strength that Journee up and moved away because you couldn't let go and accept the fact that I chose another woman over you.

Chapter 20-Kairo

These past few days have been crazy as fuck. I haven't been in the states for seventy-two hours. A nigga got jammed up last night. I can't believe Tyra played me like she did. I was with that bitch for five years she was my wife.

I'm only twenty-three and I married her. I'm a selfish as nigga but I love hard. I love my wife and I can't believe she did a nigga dirty. I gave up my whorish ways for her. Free told me that bitch was cheating on me and I didn't believe it. I went to Ethiopia for two months to check out my parent's compound and handle a few other things.

I'm came home unannounced I wanted to surprise Tyra. I brought back a shit load of diamonds for her. I smuggled the diamonds back over here. Imagine my surprise when I walked in our home and I caught this bitch in our bed getting back shots from a nigga. I damn near lost my fucking mind when I witnessed that shit.

I blanked out and I put that nigga to sleep with my bare hands. Tyra called the police and they came an arrested me for manslaughter. I got out immediately because this was my home and he was an intruder but

Gwinnett County had to smack the cuffs on me because I was black man getting paid. I pushed weight but that was for fun.

Every brick that I pushed I cleaned that shit with storefronts. I owned a bakery, two Laundromats and Taxi company and also owned a Jackson Hewitt Franchise. I can't even look at this bitch, she can have the house. I could never lay my head there. She fucked a nigga where I lay my head at.

***

Finally, I was released my brother Free was waiting on me when I stepped out of the jail. I had a condo in Lawrenceville. Free went to my house and got all my shit. If I went back there I would be liable to kill Tyra and the bond that our family shared would be salvaged because their daughter was a hoe.

Don't let these tough as niggas fool you. If a female cheat on a nigga they have feelings too.

"Bruh, get out of your feelings. I know that's your wife but the best way to get over your wife is replace her." My brother Free stated.

"Free I'm divorcing Tyra and I'm not thinking about another female just this paper that I'm chasing. My paper has always been faithful that's the only bitch that I can count on."

"If you say so Kairo, let's hit the mall. Blow a few bands and tonight we're going to stunt, ball like its no tomorrow." My brother Free explained.

"Yeah ok."

"Lenox Mall or Phipps." He asked.

"Hell, no take me to The Mall of Georgia I don't have time for Lenox today."

"All the hoes at Lenox." He laughed.

"That's exactly why I don't want to go there. I'm not trying to bag a hoe. Hoes and I don't have shit common. I don't even want a hoe to suck me off. I like females that I can wife."

"Another wife is the last thing you need. Damn you're only twenty-three." He laughed.

"Whatever nigga just fucking drive."

We made it to the Mall of Georgia in about thirty minutes. I really didn't need shit but fuck it. I could blow some money. I brought some new sheets, pillows, and bedroom set. Tyra and I made love in my condo a few months back and I didn't want to be reminded of her at all.

I had so much shit in my hand. I bumped into this bad as female. My dick instantly got hard my stuff dropped and she helped me pick it up.

"I'm sorry Ms. I didn't mean to bump into you."

"Oh, you're fine it's ok." She laughed.

"Damn you have a beautiful smile can I get your name?"

"Journee." She stated.

"That's a beautiful name for a beautiful lady."

"Thank you." She stated as she shook my hand.

"I'm Kairo it's nice to meet you."

Journee was beautiful. My life was fucked up right now. I'm about to be divorced I couldn't pursue her.

Journee

Damn he was fine. He looked like a Greek God. His skin was bright, and very rich. I could tell that he was mixed with something. He had the deepest brown eyes that I've ever saw. His eyes told a story. He had nice rich black hair with foil curls and the goatee that tapered his face was freshly lined. His arms and hands were big. I could tell that his chest was cut. I could see the print through his white shirt.

I was smitten with him and this is my first time meeting him. My panties were wet just from his voice alone. I had to check my damn self. I was good on guys for a while now after the whole Juelz situation. Mall of Georgia wasn't that far from my house.

It was nice and upscale. I came to get Khadijah and Khadir a few things for school and some candles from Bath and Body Works. I came in Macy's to get some perfume that's how I met the Greek God. I shook the thoughts of him out of mind. I need to focus and guys were a distraction.

I went to the food court to grab me something to eat before I went home to cook. I stopped by this Philly Cheesesteak spot that smelled so good my stomach was rumbling. I placed my order for my cheese steak and fries. The cashier brought my food to me a few minutes later. I sat and ate my food in peace.

I went to use the restroom before I went home. I walked right passed the Greek God our eyes locked with each other. I used that bathroom washed my hands and made my way to my car. I placed my bags in the trunk and my keys dropped on the ground. Someone picked them up for me. I looked beside me and it was him. I closed my trunk.

"Juelz ha, I thought you said your name was Journee." He stated and handed my keys.

"It is thank you."

"Your tags say different." He stated.

"That's a long story I don't care to get into right now."

"Alright, enough about that third times a charm. It was meant for us to meet today. Can I have your number so I can call you sometime?" He asked.

"Sure." I put my number in his phone.

"Alright Journee be easy I'm going to hit you up real soon." He stated coolly and hopped in an Audi with this guy.

***

I made it home in about thirty minutes. I couldn't stop thinking about Kairo. I had the biggest smile plastered on my face. I was attracted to him. I put my number in his phone like it wasn't anything. What I am doing? Lord knows I'm still in love with Juelz but I must move on.

Chapter 21-Nikki

I hate being in the middle of Journee and Juelz but Journee is my best friend. Of course, I knew where she laid her head and phone number. If she didn't want Juelz to have it than I would respect her wishes. Journee is one of the strongest females I know but that nigga broke her. He took her heart and in return she's taking his.

I understood why she left because if she stayed in the same spot she would take him back but she didn't want to do that she wanted to put herself back together again and she didn't want to face him. Different strokes for different folks but I would've showed him two can play that game.

I would've bagged me a new nigga just off the strength that he lied to me and was still messing with her and I asked you but you assured me it's was nothing. He would've felt me I wish Skeet would. I'll cut up so bad on him he'll be scared to fuck any bitch.

"Skeet I'll be back."

"Where are you going?" He yelled.

"To Starbucks, you want me to bring you something back?"

"Nah hurry up and get back. I know you're sneaking off to call Journee she's foul for that shit and you can tell her I said it." He laughed.

"Whatever I am not."

Skeet knew me better than I knew myself. Damn right I was sneaking off to call my girl. Juelz sounded like a sick puppy that's what the fuck he gets feel my girl's pain.

I hopped in my truck and pulled off. My truck was like my personal space to talk. Skeet is always up under me I can't do shit. I placed a call to Journee. She answered on the first ring.

"Hey Nikki." She stated.

"Hey, you sound good today."

"Girl I met someone." She stated with a smile.

"You met someone?"

"Yes Kairo." She stated as she smiled again.

"Damn Journee that nigga got you blushing. Who is he?"

"Girl he's so damn fine an Egyptian Goddess He's Ethiopian." She laughed.

"Damn you move on quick, don't you? You sound good though. I'm happy for you."

"Nikki don't do me. I have moved on but it's nothing major we are just talking. I met him at Mall of Georgia." She explained.

"Ok well your EX figured out you moved today and he was livid.

"I heard, Ms. Simone called me today and told me that he came by with Roses and a jewelry box that was cute but I'm good." She laughed.

"Girl he called Skeet pissed about you moving He asked to speak with me and grilled the fuck out of me. He told me to tell you that he's love you and he'll find you."

"Aw he misses me I miss him too but I'm good. What did you tell him?" She laughed.

"Of course, you know I played him like I didn't know your number. I did tell him you moved to Gwinnett."

"Call him on three way for me, so I can tell him I'm good and he doesn't need to look for me." She stated.

"Ok girl. Hold on." Journee is doing too much, she so big bad and call him from your phone and let your number show up. I can here Skeet's mouth now. He answered on the first ring.

"Juelz hold on ok."

"Alright." He stated coolly.

"Journee."

"Yeah I'm here." She stated.

"Journee come back to me girl. I miss you where you at so I can come see you give me your address."

"Juelz I'm miss you too but I'm not coming back. I'm good and I'm not giving you my address. I have to get over you." She stated.

"Journee, we were made for each other, why are you fighting this? I miss you and I fucked up. I'm sorry I love you. Let's put this bullshit behind us and move on." He stated.

"Man, Juelz she hung up."

"Nikki mane if she calls back give me her number so I can find her. I need something on her I can have peoples to find her. I'll hire a private investigator if I have too.
"He stated.

"Alright Juelz."

Let me call Journee back, damn she is doing too much.

"Yes Nikki." She sassed.

"Why you hang up? Girl that man is sorry damn he was begging worse than Lucky in Baby I Play for Keeps. I feel sorry for him. My heart was hurting listening to him beg your mean ass. God damn Journee I ain't telling you to give in but damn ain't nobody perfect give him another chance."

"Nikki, listen at you damn whose team are you on. Put yourself in my shoes what would you I'm listening?" She sassed.

"One thing about it loyalty is one thing that you never question. I'm riding with you right or wrong but I'm a real about mine and I'm going to let you know if you're wrong. I would dog Skeet out and make him suffer but eventually I'll take him back because I love him."

"That's the difference between me and you Nikki, I love Juelz I really do and we are both hurting but he created this situation. We both should deal with it. What don't kill you make you stronger. I'm weighing my options and praying for my strength." She explained.

"I feel you best friend let me get back home. I love you."

"I love you too." She stated.

Chapter 22-Kairo

It must've been meant for me and Journee to cross paths. I saw her three times in one day that was sign for me. It might be in the cards for us. When we first ran into each other I didn't think about getting her number. I saw her again by the food court. On the way leaving the mall she was parked a few cars down from us.

She dropped her keys and a few bags. I had to return the favor and pick them up for her. I noticed her ass from the back it saluted me. I wanted to walk up behind her but I'm a gentleman. I walked beside her. Our eyes locked with each other. Her rich brown skin looked like caramel kisses against mine. Her light brown eyes pierced through me. I could tell she had her guard up. Her hair was bone straight with a part in the middle.

She was natural beauty no makeup, lashes none of that. Her physique was nice. I couldn't tell if she worked out or not or just naturally toned. I was digging it. She was pushing a new Benz truck with custom plates JUELZ. I asked her about that and I could tell that was a touchy subject from her tone and her whole-body language changed. I couldn't stop thinking about her.

"Damn bruh who was that?" My brother Free asked.

"That's the pretty lady I was telling you about in Macy's that helped me pick my stuff up."

"Damn does she have any friend's sister, cousin somebody for me?" My brother Free asked.

"I don't know all of that. When Alexis comes back from the Navy she's going to kill you chill out. I'm not hooking you up with nobody. I like Alexis that's my sister,"

"Man, fuck Alexis, she knew how I felt about her joining the Marines. My opinion didn't matter. Where the fuck did that leave us, if you're stationed God knows where." My brother Free argued.

"I feel you I don't think she should've went either, but don't cheat on her. Man, up and tell her."

Journee

This nap was everything. I had to go to sleep after the conversation I just had. Nikki was trip, I love her and I appreciate her honesty. She had the nerve to say she felt sorry for Juelz her heart was hurting.

Damn do you feel sorry for me? He was my first everything that nigga spoiled the shit out of me. The way he ate my pussy you couldn't pay me to believe he was eating another bitch the way he ate. We never fucked we made love. He was gentle with my body each time he put his dick inside of me. I came on sight and body shook.

Giselle had proof and the proof she had trumped everything. He may be in love with me but as of right now we'll never know. I hate that I was so submissive to him, but fuck Juelz. We both hurting I don't think that I was being too hard on him, that's why I hung up because I couldn't listen to him anymore. I would get weak and give in.

Giving in wasn't an option. I was home alone Khadijah and Khadir went with their dad for the weekend it was just me and my thoughts. It was a little after 11pm. I didn't have shit to do. Unlike Bankhead my hood everybody was probably moving around posted up on Hollywood at the Crucial. In Duluth ain't nothing shaking.

I would have to adapt though. If I went over there I would run into Juelz and he's the last person that I wanted to run into. I had two missed calls one from my Godmother Valerie and the other one from a number that I didn't know. I knew my Godmother was asleep I'll call her in the morning. I called the number back.

"Hey, did somebody call Journee."

"Yeah I did Juelz got you tied up." He asked with his deep baritone voice that sent chills through my body.

"Again, did somebody call Journee? Juelz ain't a factor. If you want to speak with Juelz call him yourself." I hung up the phone I didn't have time to play.

He called me back I'm too grown for this. I didn't even answer the phone. He called back again a second time and I didn't answer. He sent me a text telling me to pick up the phone. I answered.

"Journee this is Kairo, I'm sorry Ms. Lady I didn't mean to offend you. I called you a few times I figured you were tied up with? Let's start over. How are you?" He asked.

"I'm good and you?"

"Are you sure? Tell me about yourself." He stated.

"What would you like to know?"

"Everything."

"Is this twenty-one questions?"

"Yeah, I don't ask anybody for their phone number, but it's something about you that has me curious to get to know you." He explained.

"I don't give my number to just anyone either. I'm seventeen years old. I just moved to Gwinnett a few weeks ago. I'm from the Westside. I graduate in December."

"Damn seventeen? I at least thought you were nineteen or twenty. You're trying to get me locked up. I'm twenty-three. What's your parents going to say about us being friends?" He laughed.

"My parents are both deceased. My mom actually passed away three weeks ago. My father died in prison when I was about four. Before my mom passed away she got me emancipated so I could raise my brother and sister so we wouldn't be split up."

"I'm sorry to hear that, my heart goes out to you and I salute you. How old are your two siblings if you don't mind me asking?" He asked.

"My sister is thirteen going on twenty and my brother he's eleven."

"Ok that's not too bad and my last question what did that nigga do?"

"Typical shit that niggas do. He cheated and his so-called EX knocked on my door to confront me and she was disrespectful we fought. It was mess. I left him right where I found him on Bankhead and Simpson Rd. Enough about me what about you? I've told you my whole life story."

"I'm Kairo Hussein, I'm not a typical nigga and I don't do typical shit. I'm twenty-three years old. I'm from Ethiopia. I don't have any children. I'm a business man. I own a few businesses. I've been in the states for about fifteen years. I'm married but I'm divorcing my wife. I came home from being in Africa for two months yesterday and my wife was slumped over getting back shots from a nigga in our bed.

I killed him with my bare hands. I went to jail last night. I'm fresh out on self-defense because it was my home. That's my life do you want to fuck with a nigga like me? I don't have any baggage my divorce will be wrapped up in about ninety days." He explained.

"Let me be honest Kairo, I just got out of a relationship. I'm not looking for anything. I'm good on guys for a while. I'm trying to focus. I can't do anything with a married man, that's a no. I'm going to Culinary School and I'm trying to learn the business aspect of opening my own restaurant."

"At least you're honest. I own a bakery I could help you with your restaurant if you would like me too. We can be friends are you open to do that?" He asked.

"I'm open to that."

Kairo and I stayed on the phone all night talking about whatever. He's was a cool guy. I enjoyed his conversation. I wish he wasn't married but I can't change the past. We click and I can learn a lot from him business wise but I got my guard up. I must keep my heart secured.

I don't want anybody to feel what it feels like to have your heart broken by the first man you give it to, but you live and you learn. My mother told me it'll be days like this. I should move on and save the tears for something worth crying about.

Kairo

Journee was everything. She has been through a lot. She hasn't folded with every obstacle that has been thrown her way she kept pushing. I love how strong she is, and independent. I commend her because the shit that she's doing those are some big shoes to fill and she makes that shit look easy.

It's funny that we crossed paths and we're going through somewhat of the same situation at the same time. Mine a little more serious than hers. Maybe it was meant for us to put each other back together again. Tyra wasn't my first but ole boy was her first.

She stated that she was still a virgin until she met him. To me she still was I bet you I'll be the last man to get it. I got her back no matter. I respect her even more because she was a real woman to leave ole boy when he cheated. She refused to stay.

She's smart and ambitious. I know she said that she didn't want to deal with me yet because I was still married but we could be friends. I shouldn't even be thinking about any female right now but her conversation is everything. I like talking to her. I convinced her to let me take her out on a date. She was a little hesitant at first but she gave in.

Chapter 23-Journee

I like Kairo a lot he's a cool person but he's a married man. What the fuck can I do with him? Just my luck a find the perfect guys and he has strings attached. Since we met a week ago we have been talking on the phone constantly. He asked could he take me out on date.

Of course, I said no. He knew I was uncomfortable because he was married. I didn't have anything to do today because Khadir and Khadijah were still with their father they went to Disney World. It was just me in this big as house. Nikki was coming over Juelz and Skeet had some business to handle in Florida and they would be gone all day she was coming over and we were going to kick it.

**

Nikki called me and stated that she wouldn't be able to come see me because Skeet and Juelz were back already. I told her that I was coming over that way but I was riding the train pick me up from H.E Holmes station. I had to be two steps ahead of Juelz if I drove that nigga would follow me home.

I wanted to see my Godmother Valerie anyway. I missed my best friend too. I knew Juelz wouldn't come to

Nikki's house with any mess. My Godmother was just as crazy as my mom and I missed her dearly and nobody was going to stop me from seeing her. I got cute today just in case I saw Juelz.

Fuck him Bankhead is my hood I'm not going to let him stop me from coming over here. I thumbed through my closet to find something to wear. I had my hair in its natural state curly and wild it was cute. I decided to wear my white polo shorts that stopped mid-thigh and a white cut off polo shirt that stopped right below my breast and some white sandals.

I oiled my legs up with some coconut oil. I needed my skin to glisten. I sprayed some perfume and I was good to go. I coated my lips with this pretty caramel creme lip gloss by Loreal it was so pretty. I decided to drive to the West End and get on the train from there.

***

I finally made it. Nikki said she was coming around the corner. Skeet brought her a BMW X5 Cocaine White. She had custom plates too Nik and Skt a hot mess right. There she goes.

"Gawd damn Journee you thick as fuck. Juelz gone kill a nigga today. You on some good bullshit I feel it." My best friend Nikki laughed.

"Who me why would you say such a thing?"

"Journee Leigh, you know I know you. What's the plan what are you trying do? They're up on a Hollywood Rd. at the gas station shooting dice in the back." My best friend Nikki stated.

"I wanted to see you. I miss your funky ass. I need to see my Godmother but of course I want that nigga to see me. I have a date later with Kairo so I'm only staying for a few."

"Correction ain't shit funky about me. I knew you missed me but let's do it. Damn so tell me about Kairo how does he look, does he have money? What type of niggas is out in Gwinnett? How old is he?" My best friend Nikki grilled the fuck out of me and sucked her teeth.

"Nikki, I like him he's perfect. This motherfucker looks like a Greek God. We just met at the wrong time I'm not looking for nothing because I just got out of something and he did also. He's twenty-three. He's light skin with big brown eyes and dark black hair and the mustache and goatee that adorns his face oh my. His bushy eyebrows are sexy. He's built nice as fuck. He owns a few businesses but I believe he does something else too. He's Ethiopian he just came back from Africa."

"Damn Journee twenty-three is not bad. The way you described him and blushed he sounds handsome as fuck. Be careful with those Africans you know they have multiple wives and shit." My best friend Nikki stated.

"Kairo is married he's getting a divorce. He caught his wife cheating in their home and killed the nigga with his bare hands. The day I met him he just got out of jail from doing that the night before."

"Damn she was foul. He might be a real nigga. He's needs to get that divorce before y'all do anything. Juelz has some competition I see. If that nigga makes you smile let him. Who am I to judge. Look at you moving on and shit." My best friend Nikki laughed.

The rest of the ride to Nikki's house we laughed and talked shit and trip how we used too. I missed my girl. Her stomach was poking out. Kairo had called my phone and asked where I was and I told him. I had him on speakerphone. He said, "Bring your fine ass back home. Don't give that nigga another chance it's my time now." Nikki looked at me and laughed. I told him it wasn't anything like that I came to see my Godmother.

***

We finally made it to Nikki's house. As soon as she put the car in park. I jumped out her truck and flew in the house. My Godmother was frying chicken the smell hit my nose. I couldn't wait to eat.

"Look what wind blew in Journee Leigh you finally came to see about me. I started to drive my ass over there to see what the fuck you are doing. You ain't grown. I miss you. You look good. I see you're having sex now too, like that thang over there.

Your mother and I got pregnant at the same time. Don't let history repeat itself. Nikki daddy and your daddy were best friends too. You heard what the Pastor said? When do you go back and getting your birth control shot because I'm coming with you?" My Godmother Valerie explained. She just read me my rights at the same time and grilled the fuck out of me.

"Godmother don't compare me and Nikki to you and my mother we're different. I don't have any time for kids right now. I have Khadijah and Khadir and my Godson that's on the way. I'm not even with him anymore sex isn't on my mind. My next appointment is in October. I went right before my mother passed away."

"I'm glad you're being responsible. You and Nikki are more like me and your mother than you would ever know. When I look at you I see Julian your father the only thing Julissa did was raise you and give you that shape and brains. Julissa ain't gone until Khadijah gone she spit her out. When she read your grandmother at the funeral.

I couldn't do anything but shake my head and pray her grown ass didn't cuss. I knew then Julissa pushed Khadijah to cuss that old bitch out nicely." My Godmother Valerie stated and laughed.

For the rest of the day we sat back chill and ate. I had fun. I missed them. My Godmother had a date. She got glammed up pretty. Nikki's dad just got out the FEDS from serving a twelve-year sentence. Nikki said he's been hanging around the house. Her mother was trying to play like she wasn't dealing with him, but we knew she was lying. It was good to see my uncle Nick it's been awhile. He gave me and Nikki both a wad of cash.

It's was time to make some moves. I checked myself in the mirror, washed my face and reapplied my lip gloss. I sprayed some perfume. I grabbed my purse because after this I was headed back to the Northside.

"Journee Leigh ready ain't it. Skeet said they at the store let's pull up." My best friend Nikki laughed.

We headed to the store Nikki parked. Of course, I was looking for Juelz. My eyes locked on that nigga. I saw Juelz some bitch was all up in face they were hugging. Nikki got out first. I got after her. She walked toward Skeet. I wasn't going over there.

"What's up Skeet?" I yelled and threw my hand up.

"What's up Journee." He yelled.

"Nothing."

I walked in the store. Everybody was looking and of course niggas were trying to holla. I was bait today and everybody was looking.

I grabbed me a water and some gum and walked toward the counter to pay for my stuff. Juelz walked in and he was grilling the fuck out of me.

"Damn shawty you bad as fuck? What a nigga gotta do to get a number or sum." Some guy behind me stated.

"I'll give it you, you're kind of cute." I laughed.

He paid for my stuff. I walked out of the door and right passed Juelz he was on my heels. I was walking fast as hell. I could feel the heat radiate off him. I opened Nikki's car door and he slammed it shut. I turned around and looked at him. My face was all turned up.

"What the fuck are you doing Journee? Are you trying to prove something?"

"Juelz I'm single last I checked you were too. It was good seeing you though. Can you move?"

"Nah fuck that, I'm not moving you can ride with me. We need to talk." He argued.

"Aye Yanica, come here."

"What the fuck are you calling her over here for?" He argued and gritted his teeth.

"Does it matter?"

"Hey Journee, you look cute what's up." She stated.

"Do you fuck with Juelz?"

"Yeah we are kicking it he told you?" She laughed and smiled.

"Nope but please get this cheating ass motherfucker up out of my face."

"Bitch you know I don't fuck with you like that." He argued with her.

I don't know who Juelz thought I was. I pulled that niggas hoe card. Tonight, I'm going on a date clearly that nigga wasn't missing me like I was missing him.

I should've locked the door he climbed in on the driver's side.

"Bye Juelz just leave ok. I'm about to start dating again."

He jumped over the seat and into the passenger seat. He was all up in my face.

"What the fuck did you just say?" He argued and gritted his teeth.

"Bye Juelz."

"Nah say what the fuck you just said. That's not what the fuck you said." He argued.

"If you heard then why do I need to repeat myself?"

"Stop playing with me, Journee I will hurt you if you think that you're about to be with somebody that ain't me. I'm tired of this little game that you're playing. What's it going to be." He argued.

"Juelz, you already hurt me. Goodbye."

Juelz

I swear I can't win for losing. I thought I was hearing shit. Until Skeet yelled what's up Journee. I turned around and sure enough that was her walking in the store stealing every niggas attention that was out here.

If she saw Skeet I'm sure she saw me. No wonder Nikki was laughing she knew Journee caught me. To make matters worse she had the nerve to give ole boy her number. She walked passed me like she didn't see me. She was playing games.

I knew she came over here just to get my blood pressure high but I played that shit cool. Where was her truck that is the question? I couldn't stop staring at her. We really have come to this. She got out of the truck and I followed behind her.

"Nikki I'm ready to go can you take me to the train station please?" She asked.

"Why you ain't driving your car?"

"I didn't want too."

"You ready Journee? Alright Skeet I'll be back I'm taking her to the train station." Her best friend Nikki stated.

"I'll take you."

"No, you won't." She sassed.

"We ain't friends no more."

She just ignored me and walked to Nikki's truck. I ran up behind her and picked her up from behind.

"Say something smart and I'm going to drop you."

I had her attention everybody was looking. I put her down and she tried to walk off I grabbed her again and put my arms around her waist.

"I fucked up Journee, but I'm sorry that's all I can say. I love the shit out of you. These bitches don't mean shit to me. My hearts beats for you. Can I prove it to you? Give me another chance you ain't playing fair."

"Juelz this isn't a game. I'm not playing with you. We've only been broken up for three weeks but I pulled up on you today to see what's good. Before I make permanent decisions on temporary emotions, but you already have a replacement. Again, it's you that's playing games. Yes, I came over here to see you and guess what? I saw enough and heard enough. So, we good."

She walked off and got in the car with Nikki and pulled off.

"Damn Juelz, Journee ain't bullshitting. I told you she was going to pull up on you when you least expect." My right-hand man Skeet laughed.

"Man fuck you Skeet."

"Fuck you, it ain't my fault you keep fucking up. I tried to tell you a long time ago but no you think you know everything. Journee ain't these duck as broads that's out here. She's not with you for what you can do for her. She doesn't care about none of that shit. She cared about you. How much bread have you came up off between Nica and Giselle?" My right-hand man Skeet explained.

"Too fucking much."

My right-hand man looked at me and shook his head. Skeet ain't never lied about nothing. He kept it real all the time. I shouldn't even be fucking with Giselle. I had proof that she was fucking with another nigga.

Yanica she fucks with everybody and my dumb ass fucking with her because her mouth mean as fuck and her pussy decent. I fucked over Journee and it's not a nigga out here walking can say they fucked her in any position but me.

Chapter 24-Journee

"I can't believe him. I swear I didn't know he was fucking with that common hoe." My best friend Nikki sassed and sucked her teeth.

"Girl, it's all good. I know you would've told me. I just needed that confirmation to move on. I have a date tonight."

"Oh, I forgot about that. Enjoy yourself don't pop no pussy." My best friend Nikki laughed.

"Bitch! It'll be a long time before I give up some pussy."

We finally made it to the train station. I gave Nikki a hug and a kiss on the cheek making promises to see her soon. I was considering taking Juelz back but after the shit I saw and heard I was good. The train arrived quick it was still rush hour. It would take me long to get to the West End. I was done moping around and thinking about Juelz.

I finally made it home. I had a good time despite the bullshit. It was good seeing my Godmother and Nikki. I didn't miss anything about being in the hood. Everybody was still doing typical shit and typical shit is not an interest of mine.

I'm sure my mother would be proud of the moves I'm making. Kairo called me on my way home. He said that he would pick me up in an hour that was perfectly fine with me. I hooked my phone up to my speaker so I could play my music.

I couldn't wait to shower and get Juelz scent up off me. He did the most today. He needs to grow up. Just last week you were begging a bitch to be with you, but your actions tell another story. I heard my doorbell ring.

I wasn't expecting anyone. I looked through the glass and it was Kairo with flowers. Damn he was early and I feel guilty for even going to see Juelz today. I didn't want him to see me with this on and smell Juelz cologne. I opened the door to let him in.

"Hey, you're early."

"I rather be early than late." He laughed.

"Ok come in. I have to get dressed. Do you want anything to drink?"

"Sure. What's wrong with what you have on?" He asked.

"Nothing."

"Come here." He stated as he stared at me very intense.

I walked over to him nervous as fuck. We've only had one encounter and that was at the mall. All of this up and personal is a bit much. I feel like I cheated and this isn't my man.

"What's up?"

"You, you saw him today huh?" He wrapped his arms around my waist and searched my eyes for a lie.

"Yes."

"Why, I thought you said you were done with him? I told you about that earlier. I deserve a chance and he fucked up his chance. I hope you didn't think I was bullshitting." He asked.

"Oh, I'm done. I saw him at the corner store and he was with another chick. He got mad because I saw him and ignored him. He made a scene that's it. He doesn't even have my phone number or my address. I rode the train because I knew he would follow me home."

"Good go get dressed and give me that shirt you got on so I can trash it. Don't wear those shorts no more." He stated, as he pulled my shorts. He looked me dead in my eyes. I could tell that he was sincere.

"What's wrong with my shorts?"

"You're revealing too much and any woman that I'm interested in. I don't want anybody looking at her BUT me." He explained.

I took my shirt off and handed it to him and walked to my room. Lord what is this man doing to me. His tone and presence alone is sending chills all through my body.

I haven't saw him since we met last week. We talk on the phone everyday all day. He wasn't just talking to me this man was talking to my soul as he spoke. I could feel him burning a hole in me as I walked away. What have I gotten myself into. I'm feeling some type of way. I have to remember that he's married.

Giselle

I'm so tired. I swear to God I am. I thought me and Juelz were in a good place. For the past few weeks he's been coming home. Journee left his ass like I knew she would. I even heard the bitch moved. I was relieved Lord knows that I didn't want to fight her anymore. I didn't beat her ass but she got the point he was my man and I'm crazy about him. We were good I fell back from Free a little.

His girlfriend was home from the Marines so of course he was spending time with her. Fuck that my cousin Keionna called me and told that Juelz was up on the corner with Nica hugged up. At first, she sent me a picture. I didn't even feel like making a scene today. I decided to let that ride. Keionna is messy as fuck too she lives for drama.

She called me back and said Journee pulled up with Nikki. My heart dropped. She had my attention. I told her to record everything. Journee wasn't paying Juelz any attention. I could look at her and tell that she was done with him. He still wanted her but she continued to ignore him. This nigga was just hugged up with Nica but as soon as sees Journee its fuck Nica.

He was so affectionate with her it didn't make no sense. He has never done that with me before. That's all I wanted from him is to love me like he loves her and I would be faithful. He picked her up in front of everybody. He didn't give a fuck who was out there he was making a statement that she was his no matter what and I didn't like that shit.

The sight alone makes me sick to my stomach. I saw enough I told Ashley I was on my way. I wasn't about to fight Journee again over him. I wasn't about to fight Nica either maybe, maybe not. I was about to clown Juelz. I'm tired of him cheating and slanging his dick where ever he could but it's cool for him to come in my bed and fuck me when he wants too.

I'm pregnant it's either Juelz's or Free's. It doesn't matter to me because my child will be taken care of regardless. I prefer Juelz to be father, because I stopped taking my birth control pills to trap him, when I found out he was fucking with Journee. I don't play that shit.

Free wanted me to have his first child also. He was willing to take care of me he wanted me to leave Juelz alone. I would if he left his longtime girlfriend. Until then this cat between my legs was free play.

***

I was so pissed. It took me about twenty minutes to get to the West Side from where I live. I don't think Juelz has ever gotten me this upset. I pulled up threw my car in park and hopped out. Even though I had Vaseline on my face I had the prettiest brown skin ever. I refused to get a scratch or any blemishes on my face.

Juelz wasn't driving his Benz he was in his Range Rover that I knew nothing about. Keionna made sure to fill me in on that. I walked toward his Range Rover and Skeet locked eyes with me and approached me pushing me back toward my car.

He wasn't stopping me, last, I checked he didn't fuck with me he was team Journee and he can continue to be.

"Let me go Skeet let me catch him. What more can he do to hurt me? Let me see him with my own eyes." I cried.

"Giselle, why do want to get your feelings hurt? Baby girl, go on home. He ain't worth it. That's my nigga but he's young and having fun. He ain't ready yet. I don't want to see you crying over him making a scene while the bitches and niggas on the block." His right-hand man Skeet stated.

"Skeet I don't give a fuck. I am doing me too I know he told you but you ain't about to stop me from catching him not today. I'm a big girl I can handle it. Remember Journee beat my ass and I was laid out on her porch and you didn't help me. Why do you care now? Excuse you."

I walked over to Juelz truck and snatched his door open it was unlocked and Yanica was giving him head. I threw up instantly and he looked at me like I was crazy. Do you know this bitch had the nerve to smile at me while she was sucking him off?

"Juelz is this what the fuck I have to do to stop you from cheating. I have to suck your dick on the corner? I'm pregnant with your child for god sake." I cried.

"Giselle go home, stop making scene man. I'll meet you there." He stated.

"I'm not leaving get rid of this bitch now." I yelled.

"I will quit raising your voice." He yelled.

I turned my back and acted like I was walking away. Everybody was looking. I was already embarrassed but I was going to embarrass this nasty as bitch too. At least Journee had some class about herself this bitch had no morals she'll suck dick anywhere.

A bitch that doesn't have morals I refused to fuck behind. I politely turned around. I ran back to the truck threw my purse on the hood. I yanked his door open he was still getting his dick sucked. I snatched that bitch up out of his truck.

I grabbed her hair with so much force she was hanging on. I started punching her the best way I knew how. She fell to the ground. I kicked her a few times in her face and stomach. I grabbed my purse of the hood of his truck and walked off. I just wanted to make a statement.

"Giselle, I told you I was coming." He yelled as he attempted to run after me.

"Don't bother keep doing what you were doing. I'll find a dick to suck." I laughed.

I can't be doing all of this. I've never had these many issues fucking with him. It's like he doesn't even care. As soon as I show out he wants to run up behind me. I still feel like shit.

Chapter 25-Kairo

I am not going lie. I'm selfish as nigga and a jealous as nigga. I love hard. If I give any female my heart, she means something to me. It's not a female out here breathing that could take that from her. I gave Tyra my heart and she played with that shit.

It's a new day and my heart is up for grabs and Journee is first in line, shit the only one in line. If I want something I'm damn sure going to get it. It's not a man out here breathing that can stop me. It's something about Journee Leigh Armstrong.

I want her. It's not about the pussy or none of that. I'm feeling her young ass something serious. I have never been attracted to any woman like this besides my wife. Journee is loyal she could've lied to me about running into ole boy because we don't have anything going on because of my situation.

I was waiting on her to tell a lie but shit she kept it real. I respected her for that. I'm going to have to speed up my divorce because if I'm married she's up for grabs. The only thing Tyra could keep was the house and car she gets nothing from me. Journee had a nice house.

I looked around I was impressed she was smart as fuck. She rented out her mom's house and got another one for residual income. What seventeen-year-old you know that's doing it like that? I need her on my team. She walked down the staircase. I met her halfway. My mouth dropped she was fly as fuck. She could've wore the shorts but the way this dress snatched every curve she had. I'm liable to murder any nigga looking.

"What's wrong why are you looking at me like that? She asked.

"You're beautiful that's all and I'll fuck around and catch a charge behind you."

"Kairo Hussein, stop it please." She blushed and laughed.

"I'm serious, since when are we on a first and last name basis?"

"I like the way it sounds, that's all."

"What about Journee Leigh Hussein, do you like how that sounds?"

"To be honest I like the way it sounds BUT someone else is wearing that title as of right now. How it sounds doesn't matter." She explained.

"Trust me the whole situation is a wrap my attorney has already drawn the papers up. She's about to be served. Look." I pulled up the email attachment in my phone so she could see what my attorney sent over.

"Dang it's really a wrap huh? You don't think that you guys could've worked it out? You're just walking away like that?" She asked.

"Let me be honest with you Journee. I'll never lie to you. If I should tell you any lies than I'm not the man for you. I love my wife I still do. I've been with Tyra since I was seventeen she wasn't my first but I was hers.

My wife had my heart anything that she wanted she could have saying no was never in my vocabulary. She never worked a day in her life. I'm a provider that's what I do I provide. I visit Africa frequently my parents live there. This last trip I was gone for two months. I brought back a sack full of diamonds.

I smuggled them back over here. I was taking Federal chances bringing that shit back, but she said she wanted some so I got them. Imagine my surprise catching her being with another man that's not me. In my opinion, she didn't give a fuck about me if she was comfortable to have another man in my home. I may be young but I put my blood sweat and tears into the shit that I've acquired on my own.

If I had any interest in forgiving my wife and taking her back I wouldn't be here. I would've never asked you for your phone number."

"I understand I'm sorry you went through that. You seem like a good guy. It gets greater later." She stated.

"Oh, I know it gets greater later I met you the next day."

"Here you go." She laughed and hit my arm.

"I'm serious let's go so we can eat."

"Kairo, look what time it is we have waited too late to go somewhere? I can cook if you want me too. I intended on making me a Philly Cheesesteak earlier." She stated.

"I don't eat everybody's cooking. How about I cook for you and you cut the onions and peppers and make the bread."

"That makes two of us and I don't like anybody cooking in my kitchen but me."

"Alright I'll let you do you, since I'm a guest in your home."

I can't even remember the last time Tyra cooked. We ate out on the regular. Journee was really making it hard for me not to resist her. I watched her as she moved around her kitchen. I could tell that she was natural. She cut up fresh potatoes. The aroma of the steak and peppers smelled good. I sat back and watched her do her thing.

"Kairo Hussein, I'm going to change my clothes I'll be back." She laughed.

"Alright."

Journee

Man, I felt bad for Kairo. Maybe it was meant for us to meet. We went through the same exact thing. I don't understand females and men. If you have something good why fuck it up? She was stupid this nigga was smuggling diamonds for you. I couldn't wait to tell Nikki how dumb this chick was.

She didn't even work. He seems like he's a real nigga. I like him I can't lie but he needs to get that divorce. I can't fuck with a married man separated or whatever. I put my pajamas on. It was after 9:00pm. The food was almost finished. I just had to drop the potato wedges. I went back downstairs so I could drop the potato wedges. I put the bread in the oven.

"Kairo Hussein, what all do you want on yours?"

"Everything." He stated.

He walked in the kitchen and walked up behind me. Staring a hole in me.

"What Kairo Hussein? I'm fixing your plate go sit down please." I laughed.

"You know what they say the way to a man's heart is his stomach." He laughed.

"Go sit down some where please. I can't feed you with no strings attached?"

"I'm just messing with you." He laughed.

I fixed our plates we sat at the table and ate. We ate in silence the only sounds you could hear was Pandora. I had it on the Beyoncé station. I knew I could cook you couldn't name one person that could tell me otherwise. Kairo didn't say anything as he ate his food and watched me.

I was uncomfortable. Pandora was jamming they were playing all the songs too. I finished my food before Kairo I started cleaning the kitchen. He finally got finished and brought me his plate. He cleaned his plate too leaving only a few potato wedges.

"It was really good I'm impressed. Who taught you how to cook?" He asked.

"My mother of course the best to ever do it. Julissa Armstrong the Queen of all Queens. When I open my restaurant. It's going to be called Julissa's."

"She taught you well." He stated.

"Of course."

"What are you about to do?" He asked.

"Nothing lay here for a while and listen to some music."

"Can I kick with you for a minute and listen to some music too?" He asked.

"What type of music do you like?"

"Of course, I like Trap music but this is cool too."

"Alright."

I sat back on the couch with my feet propped up. Pandora was jamming. I switched the station to Monica. My favorite song came on by **Monica Why I Love You So Much**. I didn't care if Kairo was in the room or night. I was singing this song. Loud and proud I got up off the couch and started singing. You couldn't tell me I couldn't sing.

Baby It's Yours Why I Love So much

Baby It's Yours Why I Can't Get Enough

Why I love only you

"Journee come here." He asked. He motioned with his hands for me to come where he was sitting.

"Yes."

"You can sing too? I thought you were Monica for a minute." He laughed.

"Man forget you Kairo, that's my song I wasn't about to stop singing it how I wanted to because you were here." I laughed and threw a pillow at him.

He walked up on me and picked me up. This is being the second time today I've been picked up today at will. Kairo laid on the couch I was laying on. He laid me on top of him and wrapped his arms around my waist and kissed me on my forehead. It was nice gesture.

We just stared at each other. I broke the silence and kissed him on his cheek also. I turned my head afterwards. My back was toward him. I could feel him staring a hole in me. I wish he would stop. He placed his mouth on the crook of my neck. Beyoncé Irreplaceable came on. Oh, shit

I love this song. I grabbed my phone and called Juelz phone blocked. I wanted that cheating mother fucker to hear this song. He answered too. I started singing loud so Kairo wouldn't hear him.

You must not know bout me

You must not know bout me

I can have another you in a minute

Matter a fact he'll be here in a minute

"You don't ever have to play no heartbreak music fucking with a nigga like me. Fuck that nigga whoever he is. He didn't deserve you no way. Give that truck back. I don't even want you driving it. I'll buy you another one brand new." He stated.

"Thank you Kairo but you don't have too."

"I want to Journee I like you."

I hung the phone up Juelz was still listening I heard him cursing.

Chapter 26-Juelz

My night couldn't get any worse. First, Journee pulls up and catches me with Nica. Second, Giselle pulls up on me and catches me with my dick stuffed in Nica's mouth. She showed her ass of course. To make matters worse I'm on my way home and I get a call from a restricted number. The Bluetooth is set to automatically answer. It was Journee calling, my baby was singing her heart out to me. Shit she had a nigga feeling good.

All of that went out the window. When I heard a nigga in the background talking to Journee. This nigga had the nerve to say she'll never have to play heartbreak music fucking with a nigga like him. To top it off he said, fuck me I didn't deserve her. Then he said give the truck back he'll buy her something brand new.

It makes sense now why it was so easy for her to leave. She's been cheating on me. I gripped my steering wheel and did a U-turn on Simpson Rd. I just left Nikki and Skeet. They were headed to her mother's house. I pulled up over there Nikki and Skeet were sitting inside of the truck. I threw my shit in park. Walked up on the driver side were Nikki was sitting.

"What's up Juelz?" She asked.

"Nikki, give me your fucking phone right now. Call Journee that bitch played me like I was some sucker as nigga. Do you know this bitch had the nerve to butt dial me and it's a nigga that's talking in the fucking background? Fuck that, take me to her house. I know you know where she lives too." I was all up in Nikki face. Skeet had to tell me to fall back.

"Juelz, calm down my girl ain't no bitch. Don't call her out her name. She has never played you. Last, I checked you was the nigga that played her and you still playing. Let me call her and see what's going on. I know she had a date and she only agreed because of that shit that you and Yanica got going on. I don't think it's that serious." She explained.

"Nikki, don't lie to me. You're like my sister. She has been fucking with him. Look the nigga told her that he would buy her a new truck brand new and to give me my shit back. What niggas do you know that's doing it like that?"

"Juelz, you did the same thing you barely knew her. Shit he might like her. What's wrong with another man liking her? She brought her ass to the West Side today to see what the fuck you had going on but you all up Yanica face. How do you think she felt?" She asked.

"Nikki, whose side are you on?"

"It's funny that you ask because she asked me the same shit last week. When you were saying how much you loved her. I was the one rooting for you and telling her to let it go because you were sorry and to take you back. You made her look like a fool once again." She argued.

"Call her for me please."

"Ok." She stated.

Journee had me mad as fuck.

"It's going straight to voicemail Juelz." She stated.

"Juelz, let me holla at you really quick." My right-hand man Skeet asked.

"What's up?"

"You're running around out here blind in these streets. I need you to focus. If a nigga was to rob you. You wouldn't even see it coming because your mind is in the gutter. You're trying to juggle multiple women that shit ain't working for you.

Pick one if you can't, focus on this paper love and Journee will come around. You have gotten caught up two times in one day. If you gone fuck with Giselle just fuck with her." My right-hand man Skeet explained.

"I feel you. I'm going to get my shit together. I didn't mean to interrupt y'all. Tell Nikki I'm sorry. I'm about to head home.

Nikki

Journee loves to play with fire. I swear I'm always in the middle of this shit. I lied to Juelz. I wasn't about to interrupt Journee's date with Juelz's bull shit. He was mad as a fuck and he deserved that shit. She served his ass it was funny I can't lie.

"Skeet, I'll meet you at the house I'm going to drive my car home."

"Why did you change your mind all of sudden?" He asked.

"Oh, I have to call Journee so we can clown your nigga in peace with no interference." I laughed.

"Damn it's like that? Since when you start keeping secrets about Journee have a new nigga she's fucking with." He asked.

"Hell yeah, you kept Nica a secret. I knew you knew, but that's their business and not ours. I'm following you let's go. I need my feet and butt rubbed."

"Ok use your blue tooth and put your damn seat belt on."

"Ok."

I couldn't wait to call Journee I need this gossip. I dialed her number and she answered on the first ring laughing.

"Bitch spill that shit. I heard about you from the horse's mouth. He was thirty-eight hot. He pulled up on me and Skeet and went ape shit."

"What did you hear?" She laughed.

"Kairo was in the background talking and he said he was buying you a brand-new car."

"Yeah I was on some fuck shit tonight. I'm not even going to lie. So Kairo and I were chilling we ended up staying in. I cooked and we were we listening to music and stuff. You know your girl can sang and stuff. My song came on by **Monica Why I Love You So Much**. Nikki, you know I love that song. I didn't care that he was in the room.

He picked me up and laid me on his chest. We were just listening to music and then Beyoncé came on with Irreplaceable you know that was my song too. I started singing that shit and called his cheating ass blocked.

Girl Kairo was like if you fuck with a nigga like me you won't ever to have to play heart break music. Fuck him whoever he is. He didn't deserve you no way. Give him that truck back and I'll buy you whatever you want brand new. I told him that he didn't have too, he said he wanted too and he likes me."

"Journee, damn Kairo is doing it like that. You deserve him though. Juelz got an earful he didn't say all of that. Girl he was ready to come over there and murder something. He said you been cheating on him that's why you left. Ain't no man buying cars like that. I stopped him in his tracks and told him he did the same thing."

"Oh, he had the nerve to say that I was cheating? I'm so done with his typical ass it'll be awhile before he ever sees me again. I'm so over it. Kairo showed me his divorce papers that his attorney drew up. He said his wife can keep the house and her car. This nigga was smuggling diamonds to keep a smile on her face." She stated.

"Damn for real. You and Juelz need a break. Giselle stupid ass was on the block today. How about this nigga was in his car getting his dick sucked by Nica in front of the store and she caught him? She pulled Nica's lame ass out the car. Girl she had Vaseline all on her face."

"Girl I just threw up my food hearing that shit. Don't tell me nothing else about him. If he asks about me tell him I don't even fuck with you no more. This boy was begging me to be with him. He's still running game but you still have Giselle and whoever else lined up." She argued, cried she was upset.

"Are you ok Journee? Don't shed another tear over him. I like Juelz but he ain't worth it. I don't want you stressing yourself out behind him. You don't live around the corner no more and it'll take me a minute to get to you. I love you forever in a day. I got your back no matter what. I'm one call away. Promise me you'll stop crying?"

"I'm ok Nikki. I promise you. I'm deleting all his pictures out my phone. I'm burning his shirts and everything. I'm cleansing myself of him. I'm not even about to drive that truck no more. I'll drive my mother's car unless Kairo was serious about buying me something new." She whimpered.

"Ok girl. Do what you have to do. I'm going to come over there tomorrow to check on you. I'm coming early so fix us some breakfast. I'm pulling up at home I'll talk to you tomorrow. I love you and keep your head up."

I'm going to see my girl tomorrow she needs me. I should be there for her. She can pick me up from the train station.

Chapter 27-Khadijah

Journee bitch, guess who I ran into today. I couldn't believe it myself my heart skipped a beat. I know you're going trip when you hear this.

"The way you sound Khadijah, I don't know if I want to know or not. You sound real devilish." She retorted.

"Just guess."

"I don't even want to guess or imagine who you ran into." She laughed.

"Whatever, my job had an employee appreciation lunch at Houston's this afternoon. I ran into Smoke and Juelz! Bitch, both looked good, especially Smoke. I wanted to jump on Smoke in Houston's that's how bad I missed him.

Smoke and me are going out tonight. Juelz wants you to come too." I blurted out. I need Journee on board. I've always had a crush on Smoke. Journee and Juelz used to be cool, way back when something happened between them but I don't know what.

"Khadijah, are you still feeling Smoke after five years?" She sassed.

"Yep."

"Khadijah you're a trip. I haven't seen or heard from Juelz in a very long time. I would like to keep it that way. He does his thing out West and I do my thing on the East. I'll show my face for a few." She stated.

"Yes, true love will never die. Are you coming or what? Whatever happened between you and Juelz anyway? The last thing that I remember is when Giselle came to our house and you beat the shit out of her." I asked. Journey and Juelz were close everybody swore they were more than friends.

"Sure, I'll come for a few. Nothing happened. When people get older they grow closer or they grow apart, that's what happened between us." She confessed.

"Journee, you are lying and you ain't never been good at that shit. I'll just ask Juelz what happened."

"Khadijah, you sure are nosey this night is about you and not me." She sassed.

"Oh ok, well I'm about to get dressed. I'll hit you up in a few."

Journee

I hope I didn't come off salty with Khadijah I really didn't mean too honestly. I should've been more enthused. When she mentioned Smoke I already knew where this conversation was going. I haven't seen or heard from Juelz in a very long time.

I made sure of that, my heart couldn't take seeing him. I've avoided him for eight years. Once upon a time he was my best friend and my first everything. He taught me how to get it how I live. Cook dope, vacuum seal Cush, weigh pills.

We used to trap together let me stop reminiscing about this man but he was everything to me. I'm forever grateful for him. When my mother passed away I was only sixteen he was there for me. He made sure I survived, stayed in school. I could take care of myself, and provide for Khadijah and Khadir.

My mom was ill when she passed away, she made sure that I was emancipated she refused to have my brother and sister split up. I'm not even surprised that Khadijah was still feeling Smoke it's been eight years since I moved us from the Westside of Atlanta to the Northside.

The move was hard on her I took her away from everything that she knew. I wanted my sister to be able to adapt in any environment. I wanted more for her than the public-school system that our community had to offer. She hated me for that but she's thankful for it now. I was going to enjoy tonight; I need to call Nikki to see if she wants to come also.

"What Journee? Khadijah already called me and told me what the move was, I was waiting on you to call me, I guess you're over there reminiscing and stuff." She laughed.

"Oh, really y'all some sneaky hoes, I don't trust this shit at all."

"Journee you're my best friend almost like my sister, you were in love with Juelz and he was in love with you too. Giselle fucked that up." She reminded me.

"Nikki, you swear you know me. I'm not thinking about Juelz that's old news. I never look back or check my rear view, besides you know I'm with Kairo and I love me some him, and I'm sure Giselle is still lurking in the shadows." I sassed. If don't nobody know me Nikki does for damn sure.

"Journee, let me keep it real with you. I like Kairo for you but he ain't it, Juelz that's your soul mate. Y'all two are meant for each other after tonight your whole life is about to change. Fuck Giselle, that bitch knows she can get it, I don't care about you stepping on her toes. I owe that bitch a beat down any way " She ranted.
"I'm too old to be fighting hoes over some dick that ain't faithful I'll pass."

"Journee, you need to stop playing games and get your man back."

"I hear what you are saying trust me I do, Nikki I'm not on that bullshit no more, I'm not stepping on anybody's toes for a man that's not my husband. The same way you gain them is how you lose them. If it's meant to be it'll be." I pleaded. I don't play that away. I don't have too, I'm already nervous about this shit because, I haven't saw Juelz in a very long time.

"Alright we'll play that shit how it goes for now but I want you two together." She laughed.

"Oh Lord here you go."

"Journee, you know how I get down. I want you two together." She stated.

"Nik, I know you, please stop because you play all day. I would hate to beat Giselle's ass because you're messy. I'm about to get dressed and I'll meet you guys there. Please don't get me in any mess." I laughed. I'm in love with Kairo.

Smoke

Juelz and I were riding through the city blowing. I couldn't get Khadijah out of my mind. It's been a long time coming. I haven't seen her in years. I looked forward to being in her presence tonight.

"Khadijah got you gone and you haven't even smelled the pussy." My brother Juelz laughed.

"Whatever."

"I can't wait to see Journee it's been too long." My brother Juelz stated.

"Juelz, man I know you ain't talking shit, you know the real reason you won't marry Giselle is because of Journee, you have hope that one-day y'all get your shit together." I laughed. He got it bad.

"Yeah, whatever I'm not thinking about Journee it'll be good seeing her." My brother stated.

"All right keep telling yourself that."

Juelz has never been a good liar. He knew damn well he was sick when Journee left his ass without trace. He's been smiling the whole time since we ran into Khadijah and she stated that she could get Journee to come out.

Juelz

Journee is heavy on my mind since we ran into Khadijah. I've been looking for her high and low these past few years and we've never crossed paths. Atlanta is small I knew we would eventually run into each other.

I knew she was hiding from me. I heard she owned her own restaurant Khadijah was telling it all. I know I fucked up what he had because before we took it there we were best friends.

Khadijah showed me a few pictures of Journee she still looked the same. If I saw her I would still recognize her. I hope she comes out tonight. Damn I missed the shit out of Journee. I guess the saying is true you don't miss a good thing until it's gone. She left me and never looked back. She's one female that I could never shake.

Chapter 28-Journee

I soaked in the tub for over an hour. I had to give myself a pep talk. I've been moping around for over an hour, trying to figure out how I could get out of hanging with Khadijah and Nikki tonight. Kairo and I didn't have any plans, he was away on a business trip.

I thumbed through my closet and found the perfect white body-con dress that shows my stomach and I paired my dress with a pair of Gold Giuseppe Zanotti opened toed sandals, my sandals were brand new, tonight was perfect for me to break them in because my nerves were a wreck.

I loved the way they accentuated my calves. My hair was flat ironed bone straight; my blonde highlights were freshly done. I colored my hair myself this morning. I didn't need any make up. I keep a natural face no beat. I painted my lips with a mac nude lipstick.

My perfume of choice tonight would be Dolce Gabbana, The One. Nikki already sent me two texts to see if I was really coming. I shot her a text back with the rolling eyes emoji and middle finger emoji. I was prepared to leave my home for a few hours.

I wasn't staying out all night and Khadijah wasn't either; she has work in the morning. It was nice outside tonight. I hopped in my 2017 Lexus LC500 Coupe Convertible. Club Kapture wasn't that far from my house, that's where I was meeting them at.

*****

I finally made it to Kapture. I valet parked my car. I refused to get a scratch on this Lexus. I made my way in the club, it was a little hood, but I loved hood, that's my preference.

It's a nice spot. I think I'm overdressed but oh well. I don't even go out like that because I'm so busy with running my business, but when I do, I let my hair down and toss back a couple of shots and it's on.

I approached the bar. I needed a shot of Patron with salt around the rim. I scanned the club to look for the VIP area after I tossed my shot back. Some guy approached me trying to chat, he was cute but I'm exclusive with Kairo I don't entertain other men period, that's one of the reason's I didn't want to come here tonight.

I'm not single and I don't fucking mingle but that's none the less I'm here for Khadijah and Nikki that's it.

Kairo would kill me if knew I was out tonight slaying for the occasion like I was single and shit.

I made my way toward the VIP area. Khadijah's grown ass was so busy in Smoke's face she didn't even see me. I tapped her on her shoulder and said hey you she jumped. I couldn't do anything but laugh. I gave Smoke a hug, dapped Skeet up and flipped a bird at Nikki. Juelz must be gone thank God won't he do it.

Smoke

Journee, thought she was slick coming late hoping to avoid Juelz, I watched her glance the section looking for him, and she had the biggest smile on her face when she didn't see him. I shot his ass a text to let him know he has action VIP, he'll be here ASAP.

The two of them need to put their little bullshit aside and move on. I blame Journee and Juelz for keeping me and Khadijah apart. That's the past and I can't change any of it. I'm glad I ran into Khadijah today. The best is yet to come. We both are grown and we can do our own thing. I'm single and she is too. I refused to let another eight years past by without her by my side.

I've came across a lot of women but they ain't Khadijah I'm young but I have an old soul. I know what I want.

****

Juelz

Everybody was here at Club Kapture. Khadijah, Smoke, Nikki, and Skeet. I felt like the oddball. I was waiting on Journee she was taking forever to get here.

Giselle kept blowing my phone up. Nikki said she sent her a text and she was on her way. I'll wait all night if she's coming. I decided to move around for a few, I didn't want to be coupled up with everybody.

Our last encounter wasn't so pleasant. I should've kept it real with Journee from the start about Giselle, but I was young and dumb. Giselle only wanted me for my money and what I could do for her.

Journee wanted her own and not mine, she had ambition. Smoke sent me a text stating, I had action in VIP that could only mean one thing. Journee was in the building. I made my way toward VIP. She looked good but she'll look better with me. I couldn't continue to watch her from afar anymore. I approached our VIP section, there wasn't any need for me to speak with anybody else.

I wanted to speak with Journee Leigh Armstrong, her back was turned toward me damn she looked good from the back. I wrapped my arms around her waist and whispered in her ear long time no see. She turned around and gave me the meanest scowl ever.

Journee

I'm having a really good time tonight. It's not often that I come out and relax with my sister and best friend. Juelz, wraps his arms around my waist talking about long time no see. I knew his voice from anywhere. It sent chills through my body.

I politely removed his hands, turned around and gave him a look that could kill. I shook his hand being polite and advised him long time no see and it was good seeing him. I walked off, I couldn't converse with Juelz right now y'all don't understand. I needed another shot of patron.

<u>Nikki</u>

I swear, I couldn't stand Journee sometimes. I saw when Juelz walked up behind her, he signaled for me not to say anything. I couldn't do shit but smile. Juelz is still in love with Journee eight years later. I should go follow this crazy girl, she's hurt Juelz feelings acting all harsh and shit.

Don't get me wrong Journee is my best friend and I got her back no matter what. It's time for her to stop running from Juelz. I'm sick of this shit. I can't even have a nice dinner at my home and invite her and Kairo over because Juelz would be here.

Skeet and I are in the middle of this shit because I'm her best friend and he's Juelz right hand man. Unlike Skeet I don't give a fuck about Giselle or Kairo. Kairo is cool but that nigga is sneaky his eyes don't lie. I don't trust him and Journee knows that.

Females out here already know that Skeet's off limit. I've bodied and bagged plenty of bitches for even lusting behind him. I don't play any games behind him, that's the only dick that I ever had. I wish a bitch would. Juelz know I don't like Giselle and Journee knows that I don't like Kairo.

Khadijah

I didn't understand what just happened, we were all just having fun Juelz came back and Journee stormed off with an attitude, something happened between the two of them and I have no clue what it was. I want to know I don't like being left out of the loop.

Journee is still sneaky as fuck. I remember like it was yesterday when I came home from school and Juelz was standing in the kitchen and she lied to my face about that not being her boyfriend. Next thing I know she pops up with a Benz truck and all types of good shit.

Nikki lying ass ain't shit either, that's cool I'm not the same little thirteen-year-old girl that wanted to run up behind the two of them. I'm grown ass woman and they can tell me what the fucked happened. I don't care what Journee and Juelz got going on but Smoke and I are going to make something shake this go around.

Smoke

Juelz damn near gave Journee a heart attack when he approached her. He needs to slow down. I know you haven't seen her in years but damn don't run her off and it'll be years before you see her again. It's crazy years later he's still crazy about Journee.

Journee can put on for Nikki and Khadijah but I know she's still crazy about Juelz too. She's putting on a good act trying to hide it. I really hate that what happened between her and Juelz it kept me and Khadijah apart. Khadijah was the first girl I ever loved.

Skeet

Juelz is my right-hand man. Nikki is my wife. I know how my partner feels about her but I can't play matchmaker with them. Journee and Kairo are in a relationship. He ain't my nigga, but I'm not hooking anybody's woman up with another man because I don't want another man to hook my wife up with another man, so that's why I stay out of everybody's business.

Juelz

Journee, is still a hell raiser. I can't believe she hit me with the handshake that was an insult. She got me fucked up with that nonchalant attitude yeah, I caught her off guard but so what you know me and we haven't saw each other in years, how did you expect me act. We were friends before all of that, she can let that little petty shit go.

<u>Chapter 29-Journee</u>

I came to the bar, to get away from Juelz and I needed two shots of Patron. I didn't need Nikki running behind me. I'm good I just needed a breather she's making shit too obvious. Damn here comes Khadijah too.

"Journee, what's going on, what's wrong?" My sister asked.

"Nothing at all Khadijah, I just needed another shot I'm good."

"Are you sure?" My best friend Nikki asked.

"I'm good y'all trust me, I gave Nikki the side-eye, let's go party because I'm leaving in one-hour real shit." We made our way back to the VIP section, shit was awkward. I had to play shit cool and speak to Juelz and dip.

I couldn't be around this man for too long, fuck that I'm not sugar-coating shit. I'll be cordial for the sake of everybody that's here. Juelz was grilling the fuck out of me. What did I do wrong?

"Y'all partying or what? Juelz, you good son, let's do an around of shots."

I didn't think that it would be like this. I thought I could handle it but I can't. I'm ready to go right now. I don't like how he's looking at me.

The DJ played **Posed To Be by Kevin Gates**

"Blowing up her phone I know she see me calling her. I whipped in the driveway she done packed up all her stuff. I'm like what the fuck I can't even talk her. I ain't gone lie this pussy good I don't mine stalking her." He rapped the lyrics to the song to me. He had so much venom in his voice my heart dropped.

We supposed to be in love

We supposed to be in love, cause it ain't no breaking up

We supposed to be in love, cause it ain't no breaking up, so we can talk about it, ain't no walking off.

That was my song I sung that shit with pride. I had my drink in my hand and I starting dancing. Juelz bumped into me on purpose when the chorus came on and looked me dead in my eyes with a death stare and pointed his finger at my head. I sung the lyrics proudly he fucked up our relationship not me. I'm over it he should be too.

"What was that about?" My best friend Nikki asked.

"Girl, I'm over it that was years ago. I moved on and it's time for me to go. I don't like the vibe and the tension between us is horrible."

"Just talk to him, you fucked him up Journee he's learned his lesson he's suffered enough. Make peace so y'all can be together." My best friend Nikki stated.

"Girl whatever."

"Journee what did you accomplish running and hiding from Juelz all of these years? You're still in love with him and he's still in love with you. Quit fighting that shit and let him love you damn I'm sick of it. I hate that I'm so loyal to you that I didn't sick his ass on you sooner." My best friend Nikki explained.

"He hurt me and played me."

"Yeah he was young and dumb and trust me that nigga has been insane without you because you got away." My best friend Nikki argued

Chapter 31-Juelz

Journee was acting all nonchalant like shit was cool, addressing me like a nigga she doesn't know talking about Juelz you good son. Man, this lady here I rubbed my hands across my face.

I couldn't do anything but shake my head. Lil Journee from Collier Rd. my heart acting too busy for a nigga, knowing damn well she was my everything and we haven't seen each other in eight years by choice, her choice, this shit blows me. I can't even speak on how I feel in this packed club but I want to sit down and talk to her about this, it needs to be addressed.

It must have been in the cards for us to meet tonight because the DJ played **Posed To Be** in **Love by Kevin Gates**. Journee was feeling herself and I bumped into her on purpose. She knew what it was. Stop fucking playing with me you hid from me. I'm done with the games.

Journee

I've been here entirely too long. It's time for me to roll. I said my goodbyes to everybody promising to link up soon. I couldn't dig in Khadijah's ass like I wanted to tonight but I will tomorrow. I didn't see Juelz anywhere around. I guess he left.

I walked toward the entrance of the club. I grabbed my key fob out of my clutch. I couldn't move because a car had me blocked in.

"Excuse me sir, could you tell the driver of this car to move, I'm trying to get out."

"Sure, it's my boss's car, he'll be out in a minute." He stated.

I sat in my car and played with my phone waiting on the owner of this car to come and move his car so I could leave.

Juelz

I left out early, Nikki already told me that Journee was dipping in an hour. I asked Nikki what type of car was Journee driving, she advised a Lexus Coupe, it was easy to find. I parked in front of her car on purpose.

I sat in the backseat of my car and watched Journee from a far. She was so busy on her phone she didn't notice me tap her window. She looked up and smiled.

"What's up Juelz?" she sassed as she raised down the window.

"Unlock the door and let me in."

"No, I'm not. What's up Juelz, is that your car that has me blocked in?" She smiled and sassed.

"Journee, you've always been a very smart girl, let me ask you this, why are you acting all nonchalant towards me, minus the bullshit we've always been good."

"Juelz, I'm not acting nonchalant, you can't be walking up on me in the club like you're my man. I'm in a relationship, I respect what we have so yeah, I'm going to be apprehensive. I'm sure Giselle wouldn't want me to do that to you." She sassed.

"I respect that, I'm sorry I'm not trying to break up your happy home YET. Let me ask you this why did you run off on me and never look back and cut off all communication?"

"Juelz that was eight years ago, do you really want to talk about this right here right now, because I don't." She stated.

"I do; I don't have nothing but time."

"Not tonight Juelz another day, please." She pleaded.

"No Journee, today I haven't seen you in eight years, do you know how long I've waited to have this conversation with you. I'm not prolonging this anymore, you owe me an explanation right now. I don't give a fuck what you have to do, but I need an explanation now."

"Juelz really in the club parking lot at 2am." She pouted.

"We can talk where ever you want, I don't care what time it is but we are going to talk tonight."
"Juelz, I have to go home. I can meet you tomorrow and we can talk about whatever." She pleaded.

"Journee, stop bullshitting me, I know you, hit ole boy's jack and let him know you'll be home in a few hours, straight up, come on ride with me, I'm not asking you I'm telling you, get out the car and let's go."

Journee

I wish Juelz would just let this shit go. I moved on, at this point nothing that I said mattered. I got out of my car and got in the car with him. I slammed the door and looked out the window. "Where is Giselle because I need to go home?"

"On your mind and not mine." He laughed.

I can see now that nothing has changed in the past eight years. He's still arrogant and cocky. Kairo would kill me if he knew that I was getting in the car with another man. He has eyes everywhere. How could I explain this shit? My Ex magically appeared when you're out of town on business and I'm in the car riding with him at 2:00am. Jesus be a fence.

What could Juelz possibly have had to say now, that will make a difference now that didn't make a difference then? I'm sorry was all I got and I accepted and moved on. Why does everybody act like I'm in the wrong because I'm not and I really don't want to talk about the past.

Juelz

I had to put some pressure on Journee. I knew her better than she knew herself. I don't care about her having an attitude. Journee had her lips poked out and shit because I made her get in the car with me. I busted out laughing.

She wouldn't even look at me, she was still stubborn just like I remembered. I don't like being ignored and she knows that, she was so busy toying with her phone, I snatched it and threw it out the window.

"Juelz, why would you do that? I already agreed to come with you." She pouted.

I ignored her, she can talk now since I took her phone. She didn't agree to do shit. I forced her.

Nikki was my partner for real she looked out for a nigga tonight, despite lying to me like she lost contact with Journee. I can't believe I fed into that bullshit. It's all good though.

Journee

I knew this was a bad idea coming out tonight. Juelz is just mean for no reason. I don't understand why he's so mad at me, I didn't cheat and lie he did. I just left him alone and moved on with my life. I don't even know where we are going. What if Kairo comes home early and I'm not there?

***

We finally made it to his home out in Mableton. If you wanted to talk that bad, we could've talked at the Waffle House, IHOP not at your Honeycomb hideout. I don't feel comfortable with this girl's man alone, that's not cool at all.

I swear I'm cutting Nikki off, I know she told him what type of car I drove. I forbid Khadijah to pursue Smoke, I'm lying I can't deny her happiness. The driver killed the engine. I'm good I don't need any closure. I don't want Juelz.

Juelz

Journee and I rode in silence. I could tell that she was thinking about a lot shit. I was too, I haven't seen her in eight years that a long ass time and I've never forgot about her ever. She was the one that got away. It was never about Giselle; it was always about Journee.

We made it to our old spot I wonder if she remembered this spot. The driver killed the engine. I exited the vehicle and opened her door for her. She got out and we locked eyes with each other. I walked behind her.

"Umm milk does a body good, Journee has really grown up."

"It does doesn't it, too bad you ain't the man that's drinking this milk." She sassed.

"If I want too I could you want to bet me on that shit? Whatever that nigga thinks he has I'll take that shit from him."

"You're still cocky I see but I'm not up for grabs." She sassed.

She's faithful to that nigga whoever he is. I need a name and I want to know how long. I'm in the business in breaking up her happy home. I don't like how she speaks about him.

Hell, Yeah, I'm jealous it took me forever to get Journee to fuck with me it's not going to take me long to break them up.

She was made for me not him. I don't care how much time has passed my feelings haven't changed. For some reason, I could never let her go. I don't know what it was about her but I couldn't, Lord knows I tried but it didn't happen. Maybe that was my payback for cheating.

I learned my lesson it took from her to walk away from me to get it. For that reason alone, I'm going to try my luck and charm.

Journee

What's the meaning of all of this? Juelz brought us to our old spot that nobody knew about but us, it makes sense now why nobody knew because he was living somewhere else with Giselle. The timing is so off, I'm in a different place, he's eight years too late. What does he want from me?

I don't want anything from him not even the truth. I can't even offer him friendship. It took me a very long time to get over Juelz my heart was broken until Kairo came along and put me back together again and healed my broken heart.

Oh, my I remember that day like it was yesterday. That's unimportant. I've came along way and I'm not backtracking. Even though Juelz and I relationship was short I was committed to him and loyal but that shit was one sided. I was the only one being faithful and loyal.

It's all good you live and you learn I'm not the same naïve seventeen-year-old. I'm wise beyond my years. A nigga could never play me how he did. Kairo knows I would leave his ass if he ever did that shit to me.

He's a good man he would never do that to me. For that reason alone, I shouldn't be here because I'm disrespecting him being here with Juelz even if it's for his closure.

I always wondered what I would say to Juelz if I ever saw him again. I really don't have much to say. I'm speechless.

Chapter 32-Juelz

I unlocked the door to our old house, I accidentally bumped into her from behind. I grabbed her waist, she smacked my hands.

"Don't do that, I told you I have a man and I respect him. Remember you didn't respect me enough that's why we're here about to have this conversation." She sassed and sucked her teeth.

"Journee, I don't give a fuck about that nigga."

"Well I do that's the difference between me and you." She argued.

She's still mean as hell. She headed toward the living room, she squatted down and took her shoes off, and then she sat back on the loveseat and grilled me.

"Why did you leave me, and throw away what we had off an assumption, with no trace or at least hear me out?"

"Juelz, why does this even matter now? Since you want an explanation so bad and I can't leave here until I give you one. Here it goes. Juelz, you were my first everything, and you knew that. I've always kept it one hundred with you.

I never lied to you about anything. I thought you were going to be my husband one day but no you already had a life with Giselle on the other side of town. I feel like you played me because I was young, so yes, I left your ass right on Simpson and Hollywood Rd. and never looked back. I didn't want your excuses or apologies anymore you couldn't keep it real so we didn't need to keep in contact you ruined that, can I leave now?" She stated.

"Journee, it was always about you, it was never about her. I know I was your first and I vowed to be your last. Giselle was something to do, I tried to cut her off but she made it hard for a nigga. I was young and dumb and running wild, I fucked up, I'm sorry and I want to right my wrongs."

"Juelz, none of this even matters anymore. It's too late. I'm good and it's was great seeing you again, you can write your wrongs by yourself." She stated. She grabbed her shoes and walked toward the door.

"Journee, you're not leaving me again, I'm not having that shit, you know what it is, and you belong to me." I yelled. I stopped her at the door and grabbed her by her dress and made her face me. We were mouth to mouth.

"Juelz, your timing is wrong, I'm in a committed relationship and I'm not leaving him for you. I'm not cheating on him for you. I don't belong to you, I'm not fucking with you, move out my way I'll see you when I see you, have a good day." She sassed.

"Journee Leigh Armstrong, you think this shit is game? I don't give a fuck about you being in a relationship. I always get what I want. I got drive, hustle, and ambition, can't nan nigga take that from me. I'm determined.

I'll let you walk up out of here today, but you'll be seeing me real soon." I grabbed her face and forced my tongue down her throat and raised her dress up and dug my fingers in her hot box. "I miss you Journee. I miss us. I never forgot about you. I thought about you always. It's not a day that went by that the thought of you left mind."

Journee

I can't believe Juelz did all of that. I almost fell and busted my ass running to the car that was waiting for me. I couldn't wait to get home. As soon as I make it home and get some sleep. I'm hitting Nikki up for breakfast and massage courtesy of her. I must get myself a new phone he through mine out. He tried my whole life. What did he mean he wasn't going to break up my happy home yet? That's the first and last time he'll ever see me again.

"Where too?" The driver asked.

"Club Kapture."

I tried to be here for Khadijah because I knew how much she liked Smoke and I wanted to be supportive and come out tonight for her. Nikki is team Juelz until she dies, I don't know what she sees in him that I don't, but I'm in love with Kairo and I'm not letting anybody come in between that not Juelz.

***

We finally made it back to Kapture the parking lot was almost empty. I jumped out of the car and slammed the door. What if one of Kairo's partners seen this shit. I couldn't even explain myself right now. I hit the push to start button and peeled out of the parking lot.

He was being very persistent. I should've kept my ass at home. It was good seeing him, it's been a very long time. I know my mom is turning over in her grave laughing about what happened tonight.

I knew this was a bad idea. I made it home in about thirty minutes. As soon as I made it in the house. Kairo was back from his overnight trip. I felt the hood on his car, it was hot. He just made it home before me.

How can I explain why my pussy was wet? I swear I'm squaring up with Nikki and Khadijah tomorrow. I walked through our house and made my way to our bedroom. He was in the shower. I pulled the curtain back.

"Hey baby." I cooed and licked my lips.

"Damn Journee, where you been baby? You look good. Come take a shower with me so I can eat you." He stated and licked his lips.

I love Kairo, I really do. He is everything to me and I don't have to convince myself.

Kairo and I have a bond that can never be broken. We made a vow to each other that we'll never hurt each other. I cherish that shit.

Juelz

I had Journee right where I wanted her. I couldn't stop smelling my fingers after she left. Her pussy had me mesmerized. It's been a long time coming. I hate she stated that she was in relationship and she wasn't cheating on him for me.

It's not like she has a fucking choice at the end of the day it's going to be and not him. I'm coming for Journee and it's not a nigga or bitch that can stop me from getting what's rightfully mine. Journee took my heart years ago and never gave it back.

Don't get me wrong Skeet has been my nigga since day one, but he hasn't been keeping it one hundred with me about Journee. I'm a thorough as nigga and I'm a good observer. I understand Nikki is his wife but he's my nigga and his loyalty should be with me.

This isn't his first time seeing Journee and I could tell. We needed to wrap in the morning. I wrote down Journee license plate number and had her tag ran by my partner that works for Fulton County. I had her whole life in the palm of my hands.

It's only a matter of time before I make my presence known in her life. I'm coming the hard way. I refuse to continue to live my life without her. It's been a long time coming. It's my time now.

Chapter 33-Nikki

Journee has been blowing my phone up me since early this morning. She knows damn well my legs are up in the air after 12am. I'm not answering the phone for nobody. She's dying to talk to me about Juelz. I told her I'll meet her at the restaurant later and we could chat.

She needs to fill Khadijah in on what the fuck is going on because things are about to get ugly. I don't want Khadijah in the blind about nothing that's going on because she's hanging with Smoke and I'm sure Juelz has some questions.

I already told Khadijah to meet me at the restaurant at 10am because we need to have a sit down. Journee needs to come clean about everything. I know Ms. Julissa is laughing in her grave about this mess. I shouldn't have agreed to none of this shit back then, but that's my bitch and I'm riding right or wrong. I'll deal with the consequences.

Eight years later and shit is about to get real and I don't know if I want any parts of it. Skeet and I would have some problems because Juelz ain't gone stop trying to get Journee. I'm loyal to Journee and he's loyal to Juelz. It's a big mess.

Juelz needs to cut Giselle off if he's trying to do something. I don't see this shit playing out well. Journee needs to let Kairo go that nigga ain't never home no way. I don't see how she can't see he's cheating she needs to do him like she did Juelz. That's another story that I ain't gone speak on yet.

I got dressed early because Skeet and I had a family day planned with the kids later. I kind of wish Journee would've kept her ass in the house last night because, I would be in the dog house soon behind her actions. Everything you do in the dark comes to the light. Lord I can hear Skeet's mouth already when this shit unfolds.

"What you are thinking about?" My husband asked.

"Journee and Juelz."

"Look Nik stay out of their business." My husband stated.

"I wish it was that simple but it's not."

"Stay out of it, Journee needs to stop running from him and let what happens happen." My husband stated.

"You try telling her that."

"Oh, trust me I am. Hurry up and bring your big fine ass back you know I don't like my wife roaming the streets without me." My husband smiled and smacked me on the ass.

"Skeet it ain't a nigga out here breathing that could cuff me if God himself tried to spit game I'll politely refuse I'm not interested."

"Nik, you crazy you going to hell." My husband laughed.

"Shit I'll be glad to go because I didn't give God no play I take my vows serious."

"Aye man hush and hurry up and get back." My husband laughed.

***

I made it to the restaurant in about thirty minutes. It was busy for brunch. Khadijah sent me a text stating that she couldn't make it. I walked straight back to Journee's office. She had her head laid on her desk.

"Excuse me get your ass up, nobody told you to get drunk last night because you couldn't face your soul mate."

"Oh, I'm up. Bitch you set me up last night. How did he know what type of car I drove? Do you know this man kidnapped me through my phone out the window? He took me to his house out in Mableton. He played with this pussy had her wet as fuck. He forced me to kiss him and told me he was breaking up my home.

How about when I made it home Kairo was there." My best friend Journee revealed.

"I'm glad he did all of that. What was Kairo going to say anyway did y'all fuck last night? You have bigger issues than that. Juelz is a man of his word trust me he's coming for you, all of you. You need to talk to him before shit gets out of hand. I'm done covering up and lying for you. I got your back no matter what but it's time for you to own up to your shit."

"Nikki what are you trying to say?" My best friend Journee asked.

"Tell that man the truth because if you keep dodging him. He is going to investigate you all of you. You and I both know what the fuck he's going to find. Juelz loves the fuck out of you. He never stopped, please stop running and let him love you. If this shit comes out my marriage is on the line I will kill any bitch that comes in between my marriage you ain't excluded."

"Nikki shut the fuck up Skeet ain't going anywhere. Why do you have to say the perfect shit at the wrong time. No Kairo and I didn't fuck. I wish it was that simple Nik but it's not. I'm grown and I know I should do what's right, but for now I'm just going to play it how it goes. Whatever happens it just happens. God don't make any mistakes. I've always played with the cards that I was dealt." My best friend Journee explained.

"Ok a hard head makes a soft ass. All I'm going to say is Juelz isn't the same nineteen-year-old boy that you were dealing with before. He's a grown as man, he's heartless and he has feelings and you are playing on that. Think about somebody else's feelings instead of pacifying your own. If I can't keep it real with you than I wouldn't be your friend. Can you please stop being so hard headed and just listen I will never steer you wrong? Do what's right please because I don't want to say I told you so."

"I hear you Nikki and I don't want to make the same mistake twice. I appreciate you for keeping it real. I'll reach out to him and put everything out there. Where do I start this shit is complicated?" My best friend Journee asked.

"Start with the fucking truth. Please do it Journee because that nigga is insane behind you and the fact that he saw you girl he ain't gone let up. You and I both know where you need to start. I'm about to head up out of here handle your business and I'll talk to you later." I gave Journee a hug and left. Journee, she ain't gone do right. I warned her Juelz is going to hunt her down. He's going to find some shit, that's gone change the game. I just hope she doesn't get caught slipping. Good Lawd now that I think about it. I wish she would've stayed at home.

Chapter 34-Juelz

Whatever I want I get it and nobody can stop me from getting it. I'm a paid nigga so I have access to any and everything. Khadijah gave me Journee's number a few days ago. I called her a few times she didn't answer at all and then suddenly, her number was changed.

Changing your number can't stop a nigga like me from getting at you. She owned a soul food restaurant in the city called Julissa's. It's been open for a few years now I never knew she owned it.

I've never been there before but the whole city talks about how good the food is and it's on point. I haven't heard from Journee since we last saw each other and that was over three weeks ago. I told her that I was coming for her I guess she thought I was bull shitting.

I still had a situation going on but that could be wrapped up within a snap. I knew I cheated but damn I didn't hurt you that bad for you to cut me off the way you did. I feel like Journee and I have unfinished business and she didn't give us a fair chance.

Khadijah has been kicking it real tough with Smoke, she gave me Journee's schedule. Something's never change. I pulled up to the restaurant it was tucked in the heart of Atlanta off Piedmont Rd. I came baring gifts I had flowers and jewelry. I pulled in the back of the restaurant and the Benz I brought Journee was parked in the back the only thing different was the tag it stated JUELEEZ and she had some rims on it. She switched the tag up so I couldn't find her.

I've been searching high and low for this truck for years but I was unable to get an address on it. I walked around the front of the building the restaurant wasn't open yet. It was a little after 8:00am. Her engine wasn't warm so that means that she's been here for a minute.

I finally approached the front of the building I noticed Journee and someone else sitting at the table eating breakfast. I had to do a double take. My heart started beating extra fast. No, she wouldn't do me like that. I hope she ain't that foul. I had to take my glasses off. The site before me had me on one thousand that quick.

My eyes weren't deceiving me she was foul as fuck. I tapped on the window where she was sitting with so much force my knuckles hurt and she looked up. She looked like a deer caught when headlights approached.

"Let me in." I yelled and gritted my teeth.

She looked at me with pleading eyes and shook her head no.

"Just leave Juelz." She yelled through the window.

"Journee let me in before I make a fucking scene, you don't want no fucking problems with me. I can guarantee you that."

"Please just leave." She yelled.

Oh, she got me all the way fucked up. I needed some answers and I needed them right fucking now. I had to call Skeet because I would need bond money. He answered on the first ring.

"Yo what's good?" My right-hand man Skeet asked.

"Pull up right now because I'm about to do life in prison fucking with Journee. I swear to God, word to my mother Skeet Fulton County can take me right fucking now. I will kill her and bag her fucking body and wait on them motherfuckers to give me a life sentence. Bring your wife too."

"Calm down, where are you? It's not that serious prison ain't worth it." My right-hand man Skeet stated.

"Oh, Skeet it is. I swear to God I can't believe this shit. I'm prepared to do the time. I'm sending you my location now bring yo ass." I hung up in his face.

I walked around to the back, where my car was parked and grabbed two bricks. I made my way back up toward the entrance of the restaurant. I threw both bricks at the window and the glass shattered. I entered the restaurant threw the window I was angry as fuck and I didn't give a fuck.

"Journee Leigh Armstrong do you have something to fucking tell me?" I threw the flowers in her face and sat the jewelry on the table.

"Please sir don't hurt my mommy?" The little girl pleaded and cried.

"I would never do that, what's your name and how old are you?"

"Mommy is it ok?" The little girl asked her mother.

Journee shook her head yes.

"Jueleez and I'm seven years old." The little girl stated.

"Journee answer my fucking question is she mine?"

"Not now or here Juelz." She cried.

"Journee Leigh your fucking tears ain't gone save you be honest with me. I love you but I could kill you right fucking now. How do you think I fucking feel? She looks exactly like me every feature. I'm not the fucking nigga to play with. Is she fucking mine? Women get killed behind shit like this. I pulled out my gun and cocked that hammer back. I'm serious."

"Leave Juelz please." She begged and cried

"You think this shit is game. I like to make examples out of motherfuckers that try me." I let off six shots.

"Juelz no." My right-hand Skeets wife Nikki cried as she ran through the door.

To Be Continued….